THE
SHADOW
OF
ASAK

The Shadow of Asak is the second book in Stephen Brooke's fantasy epic,
Donzalo's Destiny, following the events in The Song of the Sword.

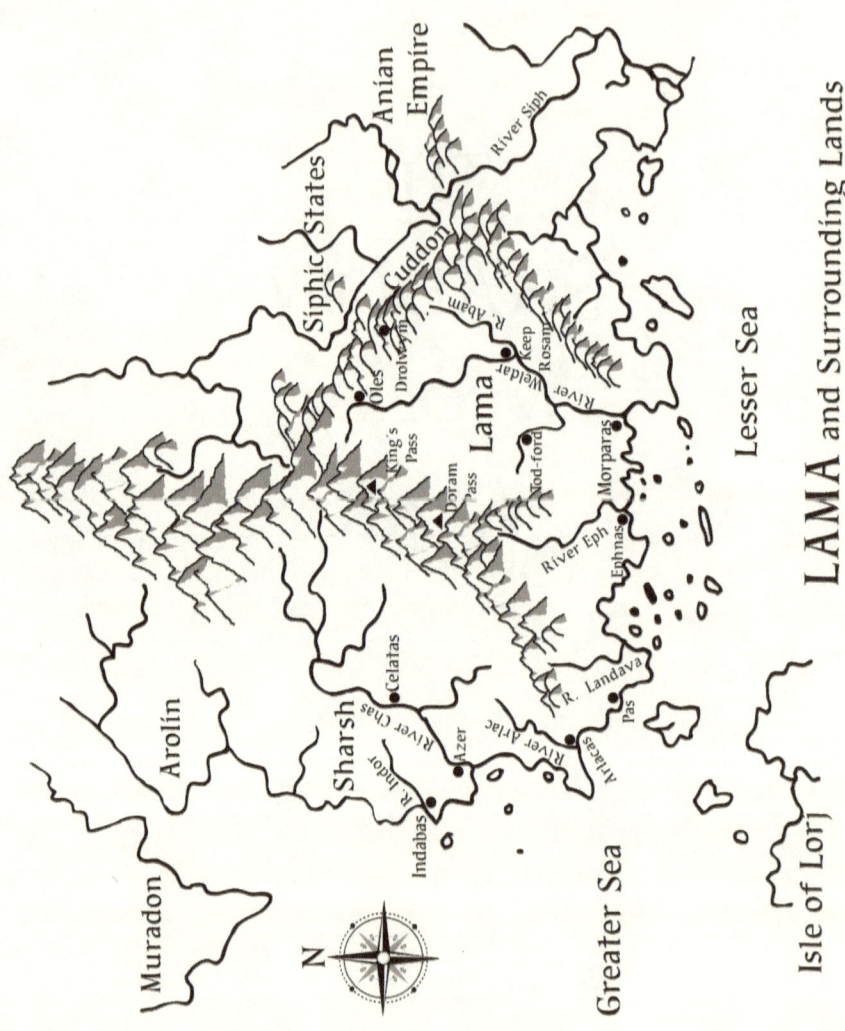

THE SHADOW OF ASAK

STEPHEN BROOKE

Arachis Press 2014

Dreams may be perilous here. Some never wake from them.

The Shadow of Asak
©2014 Stephen Brooke

ISBN 978-1-937745-13-4

Arachis Press
4803 Peanut Road
Graceville, FL 32440

http://arachispress.com

OF KNIGHTS: THE THIRD TALE

1

"When I told my father of your recent exploits, he was more than willing to confer knighthood on you."

"I hope you did not exaggerate too much." Donzalo lazed by the fireplace, seemingly half-asleep, with his long legs stretched out before him.

"There was no need, my boy. Even without them, he would have accepted my vouching for you and you are certainly old enough." Guesare paused. "Just how old are you, anyway?"

"I turned twenty while we were on the road."

"Why, you should have said something!"

"Oh? And might you have stopped to bake me a cake?"

"I would have crafted you a birthday ode," sniffed the minstrel. His companion, knowing Guesare's moods well by this time, recognized that it was but a show of mock indignation.

"In truth," admitted Donzalo, "I lost track of the days while we journeyed and would not have known quite when it fell."

"Then we could celebrate right now. And I will certainly compose something for your dubbing."

"There has been celebration enough since we arrived. It seems you Cuddonians have naught more to do with your time than spend it in endless feasting!"

"'Tis that time of year. Truly, though, young Donzalo, in this weather what else is there to do but eat and drink and sing? And," Guesare continued, "we are not yet to the Yuletide. Then shall you see some true feasting!"

The younger man nodded, somewhat absently. "So that will be the day I am knighted?"

"Indeed. First thing in the morning — what better time than at the birth of a new year?" The bard smiled broadly and stroked his curling, golden beard. "Alas, you shall have to fast the day before and then keep vigil in a frigid temple. There are definite advantages to receiving ones spurs during the warmer months."

"Then I'd best fortify myself this fortnight and be prepared," replied Donzalo. "How about another pitcher of wine?"

~ ~ ~

Lord Radal looked eastward from his sanctuary, high in a dark stone tower of the Mountain Keep. He had waited long for the return of his servant-demon, the Rupa. He had called to her across the leagues but there came no answer.

Nor was the mage Sabatare to be found by the elemental spirits he had sent searching. Things must have gone very much wrong.

Radal was frustrated. This was unusual for a man so accustomed to being in control of both his own self and the world around him. Every effort to separate Donzalo from his life, to remove the threat he presented, had fallen short.

For this, the sorcerer blamed himself. He had consistently under-estimated the abilities of his enemies. True, he was at a disadvantage attempting to operate at such a distance, using what tools were available. Perhaps it was time he took care of the young Rosam personally.

Ah, but was this undertaking destined for failure? If so, he was all the more a fool and all the more to be blamed for continuing. Radal drew his robe of sable around him and turned from the parapet. Night was cold here, high in the pass between Sharsh and Lama.

He had seen Sir Blen ride in as the shadows of the mountains crept down across the castle. Reporting to the king — Lord Radal did not like being left out of that conversation. Perhaps he should have his own talk with this Blen before the man returned into the east.

~ ~ ~

Perdos had caught sight of the fire from some distance. Dismounting, he led his horse quietly toward the light, one hand on the sword loosened in its scabbard. Whoever camped ahead was being none too cautious, caring neither about their flames being seen nor their voices being heard.

Drawing closer, he recognized the two men sprawled by the blaze as members of Sojel's band. He could not put names to them. He did not care. They passed a wine-skin back and forth.

Beyond them huddled a naked woman, shivering against the cold.

"Ho, the camp!" called the tall Laman, remaining hidden in the darkness of the woods.

The two stumbled to their feet at the greeting. "Who goes?" barked the shorter of the two, a paunchy fellow with a red, ulcered nose. The other had his sword out and was holding it unsteadily before him.

"One of your companions in arms." The knight decided to gamble on their ignorance and stepped forward. "It is I, Perdos."

The two looked at him a moment, unsure as to why this man should be here. Then the taller shrugged and lowered his sword. "Come have a drink, man. Where have you been? We thought you long gone."

"Oh, the sergeant, um, sent me to scout to the north. How went your raid?"

"Badly," spat the other. "No loot for us and Sojel didn't get what he was looking for either." He squinted at Perdos. "Are you heading to report to the sergeant?"

Perdos nodded. "Well then," continued the man, "you can come with us in the morning. He left us behind to keep an eye on the keep while he withdrew with the rest of our band." He leered at their captive and wiped his nose. "We found this one in the woods. Ran away when we attacked, I reckon, and she's given us a bit of enter-tainment while we waited around here."

His companion grinned widely, displaying a mouth full of black teeth. "We can have some more fun with her tonight before we have to get rid of her," he said. "But wine first."

The knight tied his horse to a branch and squatted by the fire with the two ruffians. The woman, half-hidden in the shadows, stared at him, eyes filled with overwhelming despair. Perdos took the proffered wine-skin but did not drink deeply before passing it back.

"Where are you meeting the company?" he asked.

"Our rendezvous is west of here," replied the paunchy fellow, "that high hill near the second ford. You know the spot." Perdos gave a barely perceptible nod. "I figure the sergeant will disband us and send us on our ways. No booty and the cold of winter coming. That's hard." Rising to his feet, he took a long pull on the wine and passed it to the other. "I want some of that," he slurred, stumbling toward their captive and pulling up his kilt.

The taller man snickered. "You can have a turn when we're through," he told Perdos and turned toward his companion who was lowering himself onto the bound, struggling woman. Then, he spoke no more but gurgled his life out, throat slit. The other barely had time to come to his feet, his eyes darting wildly in search of a weapon, before a dagger plunged into his gut. He slid off the weapon to writhe a few seconds and then lay still.

The woman cringed as Perdos approached, bloody blade in hand. "Hold still, girl," he ordered, as he cut the bonds from her wrists. "I'll do you no harm."

Hard man though Perdos might be, and mercenary, he had still a code of honor. For a moment, before remembering it, there had been temptation to join in the sport of these rogues. I'm a knight, he told himself, and I'll be damned if I'll become like these two.

He threw one of the men's blankets to the woman. "I'll remove this carrion," he told her, "and then I'll have to figure out what to do with you."

~ ~ ~

As much as it was possible for a king to like those who served him, Lareth liked Blen. He even trusted him, for the most part. This was a man who could serve his son well — he should bring the two together, when these affairs in Lama were more settled. After all, neither he nor Lord Radal would last forever.

He had listened to the knight's report, asking few questions. There was little need for them.

"Well done." The king lifted a bronze hand-bell from his desk and rang for a servant. "Bring us wine," he ordered. The man bowed and wordlessly left the room. "Blen, join me by the fire."

The two settled into high-backed wooden chairs as Lareth's man returned, bearing a pitcher and two chased goblets. "Leave it," said Lareth. The silent servitor placed the wine between them and slipped from the room, carefully closing the massive door behind him. "Will you pour, Sir Blen?" asked the king.

"How soon do you wish to return to Lama?" the monarch queried, taking the cup Blen offered him. "You are certainly welcome to remain here a while and throw off your road weariness."

"I had hoped, your highness, to return to Castle Rosam before the Yule. That does not leave me much time to travel."

"I know how quickly you can make that journey, Blen, with fresh horses along the way. Your days of service as a courier have not been forgotten." Lareth smiled, remembering the man's reluctance to leave that post. "Still, there is no point in pushing yourself needlessly."

"Then, sire, I shall start back tomorrow. If you have no further need of me here." Blen sipped his wine. It was a fine Arolin red, the best he had tasted in many months.

"Very well. Continue as you have and send regular dispatches to me. We shall not see each other again for some time, while you remain busy preparing for the arrival of our ambassador. Young Nafal must come to us in the spring and fetch Lord Doufan.

"This will be the third embassy of Sharsh in Lama. We have long had a presence in Oles and, more recently, Morparas. Both of those cities are doors to the East but the Rosam are the key to Lama itself."

"Yes, highness, they are a balance to the power of Orgelo in County Arvaram."

Lareth gave him an approving nod. "Do not underestimate this Doufan when he arrives. In some ways, he is not unlike you, Blen, a man of discretion and quiet capability. But he is also an opportunist with no great loyalty to any man or party."

The king put down his cup. "I shall leave on the morrow, as well, back to Celatas. A king must occasionally visit his capital. As well," he sighed, "as his family."

2

Donzalo was not quite sure whether the name Drolwym referred to this shabby keep or to the lands surrounding it. Maybe both, he mused. The keep of Drolwym rambled along a ridge, walls laid out with no apparent sense of design, towers jutting where they would.

The Thane of Drolwym, Guesare's father, had paid his guest little attention since they had ridden in, weary from their long journey up the backbone of the Cuddon. That was apparently to change, for the call had come to attend Vantare in his chambers.

"Father was giving you time to recuperate, that's all," claimed Guesare. "Don't be put off if he seems unfriendly. It's just his way."

They ascended a stair of rough-hewn timber, darkened with age. "Then, good Guesare, I take it son and father are unalike?" Donzalo spoke half-jestingly.

The minstrel stopped climbing and turned to his tall companion. "Quite unalike, Donzalo. But the thane is a good man. Better than his son, maybe." He began to climb again and the two spoke no more until they stood outside Vantare's door.

A huge man waited by the entry. "Brother Guesare!" he bellowed and embraced the bard in a bear hug.

"Ourru," gasped Guesare, when his brother released him. "This is our kinsman Donzalo, from Lama. A Rosam," he added as further explanation.

"Welcome, Cousin!" The large Cuddonian embraced the young man as he had Guesare. The two were of near equal size, Donzalo a little taller, Ourru thicker. Both had heavy black beards, though Ourru's was much the longer.

"Ha," laughed Guesare, "you look like a member of the family, Donzalo!"

"He does indeed! Now you will have a fifth burly brother, little Guesare." Ourru roared at his own joke. "Father awaits you. Go on in."

As they entered the room, Donzalo whispered a question to Guesare. "You have four brothers?"

"Aye. Half-brothers." He stepped forward. "Greetings, Father. I've brought our cousin Donzalo."

Having just met his large son, Donzalo was surprised that the man who stood before them was of quite ordinary size. His beard was white but he stood erect and steady. Steady, too, were the bright green eyes beneath his bushing brows.

"Welcome, Master Donzalo." The old man's salutation was formal and grave, with a trace of the Cuddon's accent to it. "Know, young kinsman, that I have dispatched a messenger to your family to tell them you arrived safely. Your father had sent word to watch for you." Then he softened. "How is my cousin, the Lady Vibola?"

"She was — well, when I left."

The thane had noted his momentary hesitation. "Ah, but growing old. We were young together." He sighed. "She was as an older sister to me.

"But we can speak of such things some other time." The thane became serious again. "You know that the news is bound to get out eventually that you are here."

"Yes, my lord."

"Don't address me as lord. We don't do that in the Cuddon."

"The peasantry would hang us from the nearest tree if we put on such airs," said Guesare. "If they could find a large enough tree in these hills."

Vantare glanced at his son with an expression that mingled amusement and exasperation. Donzalo could see that this somewhat dour nobleman and his carefree offspring might well have had their moments of discord.

"Sir, then?" he asked.

"Aye, that will do." The thane looked the young Laman up and down. "My son tells me you are both a fighting man and a scholar. More importantly, he tells me you are someone who may be trusted. I trust that you will live up to your vows when I make you a knight."

The old man turned from them without further word. Guesare took Donzalo's sleeve and led him quietly from the room.

~ ~ ~

Perdos had become a more sober man since the death of his brother. He had always had a streak of common sense — more so than the late Percos. It had been his temper that often got him into trouble.

On realizing that Guesare and Donzalo were fled to the Cuddon, where he dare not follow, Perdos had decided to travel south, find a place to hole up for the winter. He'd money enough to keep him in some out-of-the-way inn. He could wait.

That was when he had come on Sojel's men. Now, he led the pair's horses along with his own, and their captive, this diminutive, olive-skinned woman, walked silently beside him. They approached the outlying fields of Sir Paren's manor.

"Have you a husband, woman?" he asked, maybe a bit too brusquely. She nodded in reply. "Well, he need not know any of what happened to you. Just tell him you wandered about lost for a while and found your way home."

She seemed to think on this for a few moments, before venturing to look up at his impassive face. "You won't be coming to the keep, sir?"

"No. There is not good blood between your master and me. That is as that is." He shrugged, the one shoulder rising higher than the other. "But you should tell Sir Paren of what truly happened. He needs to know what's going on in his lands. Also," he added, his voice lower, the words coming slowly and with care, "let him know that Perdos — he knows the name — had nothing to do with the attack and has no quarrel with him or his family." Which was mostly true, Perdos told himself.

She dropped to her knees before him. "I thank you, Sir Perdos." Wrapping her arms around his legs, she began to sob.

"Enough of that." He lifted the woman to her feet. She stood no taller than his chest. "We are near enough the manor that you can find your way. And I must be on my own."

Perdos turned from her, mounted his horse and rode south.

~ ~ ~

"It is rumored that this theater is haunted," claimed the blond woman.

"My father says there are no such thing as ghosts. I tend to take his word on these matters," replied her taller, darker companion.

"Really, my Lady Fachalana? I thought he had regular business dealings with spirits!"

"They are as solid as you and I, but exist in worlds other than our own. Or so I have gleaned from his books when I had a chance to peek into them."

"I'm not sure but that I should be disappointed." She looked around the empty hall. "Oh well, what do you think of the place?"

"It will do, Maresta. Let's go see the dressing rooms. You know," said Fachalana, "there is no reason why you couldn't move in here. Why spend money on rent when we have this place?"

We have this place? thought the actress. How long would that *we* last if I crossed her? And, of course, she thinks I could keep an eye on it for her, as well as be constantly available to cater to her whims. Maresta knew her patroness well. Still, she realized it would not be a bad idea.

"Why indeed?" she answered aloud. "We will have to have workmen in. I see the need for repairs, here and there."

Fachalana nodded, not really paying attention. She was seeing herself on this now-empty stage, playing the heroine before a packed house. "I must have Jobo write me a play," she said, to no one in particular.

"Jobo, my lady?"

"Oh, Jobareth Nafal, my friend since childhood. He's a writer, you know, when he isn't an errand boy for Father."

The blond woman knew the name well and that she must be careful to avoid the man. "He isn't in town, is he?" she asked. "You know I met him while I was spying for you in Lama. He would recognize me, I am quite sure."

"No, he is still off in Lama being a diplomat. I don't know when

14

he will be back here again." Maresta let out a slow breath of relief. "Maybe in the spring.

"But my father will be here soon! He and the king are returning to court."

"Ah, then we had best get this place into operation, my lady. There may be a royal command performance in our future!"

~ ~ ~

There were ways into the Mountain Keep where one might enter without drawing attention. The correct password, a little-traversed passageway, and Sojel was at the door of his master's chambers. He did not hesitate to rap, using a specific pattern of knocks that would identify him.

Lord Radal himself answered and motioned him into the room. The tall man, wrapped in an unadorned black robe, did not seem surprised to see his minion. Sojel suspected that sentries had spied him riding up the valley but with a sorcerer, one could never be sure.

"So, I assume your mission failed." Sojel swallowed. It was to be expected that Radal would know that.

"Yes, my lord. It was — well, a fiasco. Nothing went right."

"Tell me of it." The mage sat by a window, open despite the cold, and listened to Sojel's report without speaking. He remained silent for a while after his man was done.

"What of Sabatare?" he asked abruptly.

"That useless wizard? He was slain while fleeing." Which was true, as far as it went — no need for Sojel to mention that he had personally put a sword through him.

Radal suspected there was more to it than his sergeant chose to reveal but it did not matter. "And the Rupa flew away. Too bad you don't know which direction." There was a barely-concealed note of accusation in his voice. "Did you see any sign of the minstrel?"

Sojel considered the question for a moment. "No, my lord, I can't say that I did. Huh, he wasn't at the keep either, then, or he would have joined in the battle."

"Yes. Whatever else one may say of him, he is a fighting man and would have been in the fray. He has slipped away and taken the boy somewhere else." Sojel, for a moment, wanted to tell his master that Donzalo was far from being a boy anymore but knew to keep his mouth shut. Discretion had always been one of his strong points. "The Cuddon," stated Radal. "Yes."

He rose from his seat. "That is no place for you to go in the mid-winter but I have other servants there." Lord Radal sighed. "I shall be in the tower all this night. Go rest. I shall need you in the morning.

"I must accompany the king back to Celatas."

3

"So that's the tale," finished Sir Paren.

Captain Corgos shook his head. "I should have remained longer, sir."

"That was not to be helped," replied the reeve. "At any rate, it is all over. Now what," he continued, "do you make of our Erlana's tale?"

The captain took a draught of his dark beer. "I would certainly agree it was best that her husband and the rest of your people not know what truly befell her. But Perdos —" He shook his head. "That is a puzzler."

"I know little of the man. Only that he left Castle Rosam under a very heavy cloud of suspicions." Paren would not mention what he actually knew of the deadly events of those few days in the spring. That was knowledge for the family only.

"He was one of Bolos's private retainers. We didn't actually serve together," said Corgos. "Same with his brother, may Kamat keep him." He made the sign of the arrow and continued. "Percos was a real hot-head."

Paren nodded. "And it got him killed."

"Yes. Both of them had tempers. That, and being none too bright, was their main failing. One could wonder, though, just what he was doing in those woods when he found your Erlana."

"I have no doubt that he was somehow involved with those who attacked us. But it's true that no one saw him here and we always knew that his quarrel was with the minstrel Guesare."

"The one who slew his brother." It all made sense to Corgos now. "Ah, so it's a vendetta."

"Perhaps that is his only involvement," agreed Sir Paren, "and I'm willing to give him a pass for rescuing the girl. I might not kill Sir Perdos on sight but I would most certainly escort him from my lands.

"Now, have you given thought to joining my service here? My master of arms is leaving me and I would have you take his place."

"I am sworn to patrol the roads for your brother this winter."

"Then we shall be seeing you here from time to time. Mistress

Tiana will approve of that — though she would more approve a permanent stay." Paren laughed to see the seasoned soldier blush at his words. "I shall ask you again, come spring. And, if possible, try to make one of your visits here fall on the Yuletide."

~ ~ ~

"Are your other brothers as large as Ourru?" asked Donzalo.

"Much larger," replied Guesare, solemnly. Then he laughed, unable to help himself. "Nay, he is the biggest of the bunch. But they are all, indeed, large men. One could certainly guess that you are all related."

"Not very closely," objected the Laman.

"Hmm, third cousins, once removed. Close enough, it seems, for it to show."

"Very well, Guesare. Half-brothers, you said?"

"Yes. My mother was the thane's second wife. I've a pair of half-sisters as well. I must admit that they are also on the large side."

The two had settled at a table in the kitchens. On the tabletop near them slept a large gray cat. There were many cats in Drolwym Keep.

Donzalo remembered something he had read of Cuddonian customs. "None of them will be thane, will they?"

"That's right. The title is inherited through the female line. I've a cousin about here somewhere who will be the next thane."

"The son of your father's oldest sister." Donzalo thought he had that right. "It seems an odd custom to us in Lama."

"But there is never any question of paternity, in that it doesn't matter. And there are far odder customs." Guesare chuckled at a sudden thought. "Perhaps you would like to be Anian and have many wives."

"Perhaps so," agreed the young Laman, quite seriously, "if they all looked like Posena."

"Ah, Donni, it is not wise to fall in love with an Ani spy." The minstrel shook his head, his expression rueful. "I know from experience."

18

Donzalo sat quietly a few moments, listening to those seated around them. Most were household retainers of some sort or another, maids, grooms, men-at-arms. They spoke in a mix of accented Muram and the native Cuddonian tongue, occasionally switching from one to the other mid-sentence.

"I should learn Cuddonish," he told Guesare. "Will you teach me?"

"Krevod," replied the minstrel. "Our language is Krevod. Your first lesson."

"Oh, yes, of course. Cuddon is a word from my own Muram." Donzalo chuckled softly. "Not a very flattering one, either, is it?"

"Wasteland. But we wear the name with pride."

~ ~ ~

Blen had not hurried. There would be hardship enough, soon, when he was on the road to Castle Rosam, so why not stay abed this morning, enjoy a leisurely breakfast?

Mid-morning found him readying his steed in the stables of the Mountain Keep. All about him was noise and activity, as the king's entourage prepared for their own journey. He expected to be off first, headed the direction opposite.

"Sir Blen," came a voice from behind him. It was a voice he recognized well. "Have you a moment?"

"My Lord Radal," he said, turning, "I always have time for the king's councilor." Behind the sorcerer stood his henchman, Sojel. As ever, that man appeared inscrutable yet exuded malice.

"I have some dispatches here for Nafal," said Radal. "Nothing very important but they might as well travel with you." It was no more than an excuse for this meeting but both men pretended otherwise.

The dark nobleman watched him tuck the papers into a saddlebag. "Blen," he said, "we serve the same master. I assume our king has chosen to employ you as his eyes in Lama. That is wise — there is always use for another view of things.

"I warn you, though, that there is much more happening than you could ever know. Stick to taking care of our embassy and keeping his majesty informed and, should you need help, remember that I am not your enemy. But do not, I warn you again, become involved in that which you do not understand."

~ ~ ~

"We call on thee, Lady of the Dark Moon!"

"We call on thee," repeated the circle of cloaked figures. Stone bowls were being passed from hand to hand, and each drank deeply.

"Bring the day when the sun is not reborn, when the new year comes not!"

"Bring the day that is eternal night," came the response. Their voices echoed from the dark cavern vault above them, invisible by the unsteady light of torches

In the middle of the assembly, on a dais hewn of the solid stone, stood one swathed all in black and holding a heavy, twisted staff. A faint sickly-green light played about its shaft.

"Sisters," she cried, "we have been tasked." There was a murmur that quickly died away. "A servant of the night came to me. As a bat did it come, to whisper of an enemy among us — an enemy of the dark!"

The murmur began again. This time it grew to become the howling of many voices, rising in a drug-driven frenzy.

"He is newly come to Castle Drolwym! We must slay him!" shrieked their leader over the cacophony of her coven.

"We will tear him apart!" one cried. "We will throw his tattered flesh to the four winds!"

"I will pluck his eyes from his head," promised another, "and make him look upon his own broken body!"

"And I will wear his manhood as a necklace!" cried one beside her, to the delight of her crazed companions.

Beneath her veil, their leader smiled.

4

On a hilltop, not so far away, stood another group of women. These women, despite the cold, were quite naked.

"Sisters," spoke she who led them, at the end of their rites, "rejoice with me. My son has returned."

"I'd best lock up my brother," joked one of the circle. The others laughed with her.

As did the handsome, middle-aged woman who stood at their center. "Yet he has brought serious news," she continued. "There is one with him who may need our protection. He has been marked for death by the Dark One."

"Oh, do you mean Donzalo?" asked a woman. "I've seen him around the keep. He's cute."

"If you think bears are cute. He looks like one of your step-sons, Lady Se," said another.

"So I have heard," replied their leader. "I have not yet set eyes on him. But if the boy needs our help and that of the Great Mother, we should be prepared.

"Now let us go someplace warm, put on some clothes and drink wine!"

~ ~ ~

Borrago reached down to stroke the head of the half-grown dog lolling at his feet. The pup was, ostensibly, his grandson's yet it had chosen to follow the count about — and the count had not objected.

"Any word from your silent partner, Lector?" he asked the young man sitting across the table. Jobareth Nafal smiled faintly at the description of his supposed underling, Blen. Count Borrago had correctly surmised their actual, if secret, equal footing.

"No, my lord, which means he is probably on his way back here. Had he been detained he would have sent a message."

"But he himself can make as good time as any courier, having been one not long ago," spoke a third man who sat in the corner, his countenance partly concealed by shadow. Until then, Borrago's master of arms, Copago, had been a quiet but palpable presence.

"Well, I suppose we've done all we need on these papers." Borrago pushed the stack of documents aside. "Thank you for coming up, Nafal." He leaned back and regarded the young diplomat for a moment. "You will come for the Yule feast, of course."

"Certainly, sir. I would not miss it. Shall I bring my, uh, partner too?" Jobareth immediately wished he had not said that. It did not do to become overly familiar.

But the count laughed at his little jest. "By all means, my boy. Sir Blen is always welcome here." He reconsidered that. "Well, almost always. You and I have secrets to which he should not be privy, eh?"

The Sharshite immediately caught Borrago's intention. "There is news of Donzalo, my lord?"

"Indeed there is." The count took papers from a side table and laid them before him. "Two letters," he said, "one from my brother and one from Drolwym."

"Drolwym, my lord? I do not know the name."

"It is a hold in the Upper Cuddon. Guesare's father is lord there." Borrago picked up the letter. "The message is brief but it does say that both arrived there safely.

"Now this other letter — between it and what my man Corgos has reported, it would seem there have been some strange goings-on up the Abam."

"Is Sir Paren well, my lord? And Lady Thara?"

"Yes. Here, read for yourself." He passed the letter to Jobareth, who read through the message, written in Paren's own cramped scrawl.

"Strange goings-on for certain, sir." He looked up at the count. "All in all, it seems to have turned out well."

"Men and women were slain," interjected Copago. "That is never good."

Nafal nodded. "True, sir. Quite true."

"But it could have been far worse," said the count, "and there was much gallantry. I do believe that I shall knight our Corgos this Yule."

"He has requested that he be at your brother's keep that day," Copago said. "I hear he has a lady love there."

Boraggo threw back his head and laughed openly. "Well good for him. Let's dub him tomorrow and he can go to her as a knight!"

~ ~ ~

"Not all my brothers are fond of me. Nor of each other, for that matter."

"Is that so?" replied Donzalo, as they entered the crowded hall. "What of your sisters?"

"The one is far away, with her husband. Her, I get along with well enough. The other — well, there she is." He nodded toward a tall, stout woman of indeterminate age. "'Twould be better were I to let Ourru introduce you."

"She seems — formidable."

"Indeed. It is generally believed she poisoned her husband. Ah, here is Ourru." Guesare sighed. "And Mausare as well."

Mausare seemed a slightly smaller version of his brother, which made him still quite a large man. "Ho, Brothers!" came Ourru's greeting. "Donzalo, this is our brother Mausare. He's the runt of the family!' He guffawed at the sour look on Mausare's face. "Our women are about somewhere. By the way, Mausy's wife seems to think you're rather a handsome young fellow." He nudged his brother in the ribs with a massive elbow.

"Greetings, brother," said Guesare, and embraced the man, not with the enthusiasm of an Ourru, yet with a certain tenderness. "Is all well with you?"

"Well enough, Guesare." The man turned and took Donzalo's hand. "Greetings to you, young sir."

"Is anyone else here?" asked the minstrel.

Mausare answered. "Habidros is still with his free company, some-where in the Siphic cities. To be honest, I'm not sure where Galaro is."

Guesare turned to Donzalo. "Galaro was the only one of us who chose to go into trade rather than fight or farm. Though I'm not convinced he quite understands the difference between trade and smuggling."

"I saw your sister a few minutes ago," Ourru suddenly stated.

"Nosana? We saw her too and avoided her." For once, all three brothers laughed together.

"Nay, I mean Jola."

Mausare seemed surprised and, perhaps, a bit dismayed. "It is rare for her to show up here." Noting Donzalo's puzzlement, he explained, in an almost too matter-of-fact a voice. "Jola is Guesare's half-sister by his mother. Our step-sister."

"Oh." Donzalo glanced at the minstrel, who was staring at the floor. There followed a moment of silence, decidedly of the awkward sort.

Then Ourru spoke. "Well, Cousin, someone must introduce you to Nosana and it would seem to fall to me. I'm the only one of us," he confided with a wink, "who isn't scared of her."

A group of children scurried across their pathway. Donzalo was surprised to see youngsters so much in evidence at Drolwym. Back at Castle Rosam, they rarely appeared at such gatherings.

Though Nosana was very tall, as women generally go, she did not seem so beside Ourru and Donzalo. Nosana resented that fact. She liked being the most imposing figure in a group.

She drew herself up as the pair approached. Nosana allowed her brother to hug her, but barely. "This is our kinsman Donzalo," said he. "Donzalo, this is my sister Nosana."

The woman stared at Donzalo a moment, as if uncertain of her best course. Then she smiled and embraced him. "Greetings, Cousin," she said, her voice all honey and wine. "We are most pleased to meet you."

~ ~ ~

Leaving Donazalo for a while to his siblings, Guesare crossed the hall to where his parents held court. Vantare was sitting quietly, seemingly bemused by the comings and goings of his guests. His son bowed to him but was barely acknowledged.

Guesare's mother beckoned him. "Your father is in one of his moods," she whispered as she embraced her son. "It is good to have you home."

"It is good to be home," he responded.

The Lady Se smiled. "For a while. You will grow restless, as always." She looked out into the crowded room. "But you have a charge, now, who requires your attention."

"He needs it less and less, Mother. Donzalo is becoming a rather capable young man. I think Nosana has her hooks in him at the moment but I'll bring him over to meet you, as soon as I can."

"Be wary of Nosana. I sense both lust and malevolence in her tonight."

"Would that I had your gifts!" Guesare exclaimed. "I can not read like that and certainly not from a distance."

"I've never heard of a man who could. You have your own abilities, my son, or you would not be here with me now."

"Lust, you say? Not for Donzalo?"

"Why not? He's a morsel I might not mind sampling myself." She laughed gaily at his expression. "Fear not, my Guesare, I will leave your friend be."

"There are too many people here and I know not friends from enemies," said the minstrel. "Maybe I should not have brought him to my home."

"You know you can trust me," Guesare's mother reminded him, "and your sister Jola, mad though she may be."

5

"They're little more than food for the swine," claimed the little innkeeper. "Why should I want these nags?"

Perdos sighed deeply. He had never enjoyed bargaining and always seemed to get the worst of it. But he knew horses well enough to place a proper value on these two — they were decent steeds. Certainly much better quality than their late owners.

"I'll not quibble," he said. "We both know they are good horses. Make a decent offer or I'll be off with them."

"Hmm." The man ran his hands over the animals, occasionally squinting or pursing his lips. Perdos suspected all of it was show. "Would you consider, say, two — no, let's make it three crowns for the pair of them?"

"Let's not. Don't waste my time, man. I want to get over the river soon."

"Crossing the Weldar? Something over there you need? Or do you just feel safer on the other side?" The sly jest came close to the mark.

Perdos felt himself growing angry but then he considered the innkeeper's question. He leaned back against a fence rail and exhaled. "I'm not really sure," he said. "Damn it, I've no real reason to cross at all. I'm just looking for a place to spend the winter."

The man cocked his head at the knight. "This *is* an inn, you know. I have few enough guests when winter slows down traffic on the river. What do you say to four weeks lodging and meals in exchange for the horses?"

"Make it six," said Perdos, "and stabling for my own steed."

"You must include the saddles. Done? Very well. I'll show you your room."

Perdos sighed. He didn't know whether he had gotten the best of this deal but he was satisfied with it. And he was very tired.

~ ~ ~

It was raining in Celatas, a light, warm rain, little more than a mist. King Lareth did not mind it, welcomed it, after the cold winds and snows of the mountains. He and his entourage rode slowly through the cobblestone streets, climbing toward the royal keep.

Celatas was not an old city. Lareth's father, King Greneth, had chosen to build his capital on this spot when he took the throne. The name meant nothing more than 'Royal City.'

Unlike the old capital of Sharsh, which had lain near the coast, Greneth's city was placed well inland. A high rocky hill surmounted the city and the king's keep surmounted that hill. Far below was the wide River Chas, which flowed through the heart of the nation.

Lord Radal had once observed to the king that his citadel was much like that of the Rosam, the same defensible heights guarding a major river trade route. On giving it thought, Lareth realized that it made sense — similar needs would produce similar results. His city and keep were, however, far larger than anything in Lama. They were the capital of a great nation.

And that great nation made great demands on his time. There would be a flurry of celebrations and balls to mark his return and simply because it was that time of year. Then he must buckle down to the job of governing.

In the back of his mind, though, he was busy laying out his garden for the coming spring. He wished that Lomela could visit and see it. Why shouldn't she, yes, and his grandchildren too?

"Sire." He glanced at the squire by his side and then at the coming turn of the road.

"Yes, my boy," he said, "I've been day-dreaming. It's one of the few pleasures left a king."

~ ~ ~

"Mausare, like his father, is given to dark moods. We get along well enough, most of the time, and I think him a good man."

"That's recommendation enough for me," said Donzalo. "I like your mother. Is she really a priestess?"

"High Priestess of Rema."

The Earth Mother, thought Donzalo to himself. That's one of the really old deities. A Kamatian he might be, but a well-read one.

"I never saw your other sister."

"She was gone already," said Guesare. "It is rare for her to show herself at all. Jola spends more time in the company of the fay of the hills than she does humans."

The two were lounging before the fire in Donzalo's room, sorting out all that had transpired that evening. It was important to both that they understand what winds were blowing through this place.

"Mausare seemed troubled when her name was mentioned."

The minstrel gazed into the fire so long that Donzalo almost spoke again.

"He had an — entanglement with my sister," Guesare said at last. "Since they are not truly related by blood, there was no reason they shouldn't, after all. Except that it was bound to end badly.

"Jola is not an ordinary woman. She has abilities, as does my mother — or I, for that matter — but hers are much greater. They have driven her to madness."

"Is her father dead?" asked the young Laman.

"We do not know who her father was. She was conceived at one of the temple, um, celebrations, a couple years before the Lady Se married the thane." He shook his head and made an attempt at a smile. "Mother insists that the father was a god. Who knows? Maybe he was."

He fell silent again. Donzalo half-suspected he had fallen asleep.

"Beware my other sister," Guesare suddenly said. "She desires you. I think she may desire to kill you as well." He rose to his feet. "And on that shall I leave you to your sleep," he laughed, and passed out the door.

~ ~ ~

"Blen! We did not expect you so soon." Jobareth came forth from their lodgings to grip the hand of his associate. "Come on in."

"I felt an urgency to be back here," replied the knight, "so I rode courier-style." He gave the young diplomat a tired smile. "I am in great need of sleep."

"I would think so. At least you have a few days to rest before the

Yule parties." Jobareth chuckled. "After them, you will need to rest again."

Blen nodded. He had little desire to exchange banter at any time, but certainly not right then. Bed was his desire, and sleep.

Yet the weary knight did not sleep when he lay down his head. Too much was going through his mind. What was expected of him? Was he to fear Lord Radal or to confide in him? And of just what had the councilor been warning him? Was Jobareth involved in some plot? Around and around the questions went and his legs ached and he could not find comfort.

As the morning sun brought Ros-town to life, slumber finally took him.

6

Nosana beheld her reflection in her mirror. She was proud of her mirror — it was of glass and the only one like it in the Cuddon, brought from the Siphic League by her husband at great expense and effort. Too bad, she thought, he didn't put enough effort into other things.

She was proud of her reflection, too. That she was a woman of appetites showed in her figure. But she was not unattractive, tall, erect, full-bosomed. Still young, too. Young enough.

Yes, she would have this Donzalo. And then, alas, she would have his life as well. A few drops of poison in his wine would do. It might be interesting to watch his death struggle. Two pleasures in one night, she laughed to herself.

Dropping her robe, Nosana beheld herself again and nodded. Shouldn't that be enough to get the young Laman into her bed? She shrugged. If not — well, there were potions.

It had been a good night, after all, and not marred by her fools of brothers. And little Guesare, despite their mutual hatred, had brought her quite a nice gift.

~ ~ ~

"I do not like this," the crown prince stated flatly, "not at all, sir. Allowing my brother to marry into that family cuts into my own claims to the throne."

"But it ties them to our dynasty," said Lareth. "Better Modareth than some ambitious nobleman." The king seated himself by a window, shuttered against the winter, and looked his son up and down. "I think you have nothing to fear from your little brother."

"Oh, certainly, Father. But marriages produce heirs." Both became silent for a moment before the younger man continued in more subdued voice. "Or it is to be wished that they will."

"There is plenty of time yet for that, Gawis. I have no doubt that you will give me a grandson." Lareth pulled his shawl closer about him. He should call the servants to build a bigger fire in here.

The prince brushed back his shock of stiff sandy-blond hair.

Lareth knew it for a habit of his when at unease. Dressed in green again, he thought. Does he do that for the impression it makes or does he truly want to wear my colors?

"Sire," began Gawis, "I can only hope."

"It takes more than hope, boy." The king couldn't help making the jest.

Which his son ignored. "This marriage in itself is not so bad, I suppose, but it comes on the heels of Lomela's." He began slowly pacing before the fire. Giving himself time to think, thought Lareth. "That makes two ties to the family of Duke Paren."

"The bride is second cousin to Count Borrago," said the king. "That is not a bad thing, Gawis. Their families would make more likely rivals than allies."

"Hmm, yes, Father, I see that. The claim of one undercuts that of the other." Gawis frowned. "Would that I could recognize things like that. I doubt my ability to succeed you."

Lareth briefly felt himself likely to agree. "You'll learn, my son. More importantly," he continued, "you need proper advisers around you — not that circle of flatterers you think your friends."

The younger man nodded but the king did not know if he took his words to heart.

~ ~ ~

"Cursed cat!" Donzalo caught himself before he went tumbling down the stairs. "It's a wonder everyone in this castle doesn't have broken bones."

The offending feline purred innocently and rubbed against his leg. "You aren't in league with Lord Radal, are you?" he asked it. "Lying in ambush on these stairs, just waiting your chance to trip me up — why you even look like him in your black coat!"

From below him, came the unmistakable sound of a rebec. Guesare would not be hard to find this morning. The minstrel was seated on the floor, just outside the kitchens, surrounded by a circle of children.

"Ah, my little ones, here is my friend Donni. I must leave you now." The group turned around to stare at Donzalo.

"He's big!" said one of the boys.

"Not as big as my dad," claimed another. "He's the biggest man in the world! Right, Uncle Guessy?"

Guesare rose to his feet. "Your father is very large but he can't compare with the Stone Giants in the Lofty Mountains. Why, they use pine trees as toothpicks and have to be careful not to bump their heads on the sky when they stand up straight." He turned to Donzalo. "That's one of Ourru's boys."

"So, you have a whole other talent of which I knew nothing. You could be story-telling in the marketplace for the children's copper coins."

"I have done just that," said Guesare. "It is an honorable craft."

"Then I apologize for making light of it. I know many stories but I can not think of even one suited to children." Donzalo grew pensive, of a sudden. "My own son will soon see his first birthday. I would be there with him."

"And I'm sure you will be. Farewell, children. I'll play for you again when I can." The two stepped into the kitchen. It was late for breakfast and early for lunch, so the tables were mostly empty and the cooks and scullions were busy with cleaning and preparation.

"Speaking of bumping ones head, I need be careful in here," observed Donzalo, as he avoided a strand of sausages dangling from the ceiling beams.

"Can you bring us something, lass? Anything," said Guesare to a serving girl. "Tell me, Donzalo, in which temple would you prefer to stand your vigil? I know you're Kamatian, but that is not an option here."

"So what is? Thank you," Donzalo said as a bowl of bread and dried fruits was placed before them.

"Well, my father would probably recommend Jov. He is the chief of the gods, of course, so always a good choice.

"Mother, on the other hand, would say Rema, who is, after all, mother of Jov. Or grandmother, depending on which cult you follow. Sometimes both. I would recommend against that as her temples are quite open to the weather. Not at all a good idea at this time of year."

"Tell me," said the Laman, taking a sip from the tankard that had been handed him, "is there a temple of Diba? And what is this?" He sniffed at it.

"Diba, the Huntress? Yes, we have a shrine near here." Guesare drank deeply from his own tankard. "You've never had buttermilk before? Drink up, it's good for you. It will help you grow!"

Donzalo gave his companion a properly pained expression and sipped some more. He might like this stuff. Or maybe not.

"Why Diba?" asked Guesare.

"She's the one goddess whose worship lives on in Lama. Only among the peasants, who tend to lump her with the fairies and such. I always liked the stories they told of her and her wolf pack, hunting through the night for the demons who might harm children."

"You see, my friend, you do know stories for youngsters. You were only looking for them in the wrong memories."

~ ~ ~

Why couldn't any of the men she knew be like this Donzalo? wondered the Lady Fachalana. Between the dispatches — admittedly, not meant for her eyes but read none the less — sent to Lord Radal, the gossipy letters from Jobareth, and the reports of her personal spy, Maresta, she had learned quite a lot about him. And to think that her father was trying to kill the man!

Well, that wouldn't do.

Her father thought his secret papers well hidden and well guarded, but while he was far away in the mountains, she had looked through them and learned the reason — that Donzalo's son was prophesied to rule in Lama. If that were so, then who was to say who might be the mother? Fachalana could see herself beside such a man. Now that would be a proper stage for her!

Ha, she laughed to herself, am I to fall in love with someone of whom I have only read? Best to busy herself with her new theater and put such foolishness from her head.

The warm rain that had come yesterday was turning to light snow. Winter was never very bad here in Celatas and there would be a whirlwind of balls and feasting to entertain her for the next few days. But her boredom would return, Fachalana knew. She would soon thirst for adventure again.

7

"My Lady Nosana." Donzalo bowed toward the woman seated before him.

"Oh, you have accepted my invitation! Welcome, my young kinsman." She dismissed her serving girl with a quick glance from beneath her dark, arching brows. "Here, join me in some wine of Dor." She poured out the golden liquid into two goblets — goblets of fine Siphic glass.

The Cuddonian woman was dressed in a black gown, cut to display her ample breasts. Her raven hair lay loose upon her shoulders.

Donzalo could see the great vanity of this woman, the showing off of her expensive possessions, the mention of a rare wine, the self-conscious display of her own desirability. He had grown up with far more wealth, yet among a people who shunned ostentation.

Still, she was an imposing and, yes, attractive person. Her tendency to flesh did not conceal the firm jaw, the high cheekbones and strong straight nose, and certainly not the headstrong spirit that drove her. She's hardly much older than Guesare, he thought.

"I thank you, my lady," said Donzalo, evenly, politely, seating himself across the low table and taking the proffered glass. Nosana allowed her fingers to linger on his for a moment, before smiling and lifting her own goblet.

"To friendship," she toasted, "and all it might bring." There was a hunger in her voice and Donzalo began to feel an answering appetite within himself. It had been long since he had held a woman. It had been even longer since that last night with Lomela, the only woman to whom he had ever made love. Ah, that he could again, just once, be that simple boy who had loved a princess.

Nosana sensed his desires, or thought she did. She leaned back into the many-colored satin cushions that overflowed her divan and gave him a frank look. "You are quite a handsome fellow, aren't you? Some might think your nose too large but it suits the rest of you. I trust your largeness is uniform."

Donzalo felt briefly embarrassed, not for himself but for this woman. Such coyness suited her not. A mix of curiosity and boredom had drawn him here and, in honesty, he had come not completely opposed to the idea of a dalliance with her.

Now, though — she seemed silly, stupid, and almost certainly dangerous. But she remained physically desirable and, after all, no one had a claim on his fidelity. Not Lomela, not anymore. Not Posena, or whatever her name truly was. He recalled the little spy's fair face turned up to kiss him, when last they were together, and realized he wanted something other than what this woman before him offered.

He sighed deeply. "This is not to be, my Lady Nosana. I must leave." Her face immediately displayed her frustration, even anger, but she quickly hid that beneath a mask of sweetness and resignation.

"Then drink one more goblet of wine with me, at least. It will help ease my disappointment."

~ ~ ~

"I am worried for Donzalo. He accepted an invitation to attend Nosana in her rooms."

"Trust your friend," replied the priestess.

"I do but I certainly do not trust my sister," Guesare told his mother. "You are the one who sensed menace in her."

Lady Se put down her embroidery. It was a design made of mystic runes that the minstrel found quite confusing. "I always sense menace in Nosana. You think she means to do more than simply seduce him?"

"I don't know. Could she be allied with those who would do him harm?" Guesare sounded frustrated. "I did not bring him all the way here so it could be for nothing!"

"It will not be." She turned back to her needlework. "I have set one to guard him. Hmm, now which shade of red would work best here?"

~ ~ ~

Nosana smiled from her doorway as Donzalo walked, a bit unevenly, back to his own room. It would take but a short while for her potion to inflame him and then she would follow. It were best done in the boy's chamber, anyway, both her enjoyment of him and that which followed — his body in her rooms might have been difficult to explain.

She doffed her gown — no need for that now — and drew a loose robe about her naked body. That should be time enough, she told herself, as she stepped into the curving hallway. First side-passage and then — yes, here it is, door ajar. Nosana laughed softly. The boy's mind had not been on closing doors behind him, much less bolting them, by the time he got here. Nosana could have forced it with a minor magic, if need be, but she'd rather not have to bother.

But she would bolt it behind her and set a seal upon it as well. That done, she turned to where Donzalo stood in the darkened room. His breathing came to her ears deep and ragged. She threw aside her robe. "Come to me!" she demanded.

He stumbled forward, eager to have her. How beautiful he is, even so, mused Nosana. She'd best make the most of him. "Here," she said, placing his large strong hands where it pleased her.

"You will not," came a voice from behind her.

She spun around to see the door open, her seal as nothing. A tall woman, dark of skin but golden haired, stood there. "Your little spells are like cobwebs to me, Nosana, wiped away with a sweep of my hand." She looked at the confused young man and, shaking her head, turned back to Nosana with utter scorn.

"Do not try me. You know you can not. Now begone!" Nosana hesitated a moment, then ran from the room, quite quickly for so heavy a woman.

Donzalo stood bemused in the middle of the chamber. As the woman approached, he reached for her, tried to pull her close, bring his lips to hers. She gently pushed him away and smoothed her long white gown. "No, no, sweet boy. Sleep and I shall guard thee." She guided him gently to his bed and stayed there by his side, singing songs that seemed to hold all the dreams ever dreamed, until his fever left him and he found sleep.

Nosana fumed as she slipped back to her room. Her robe lay on Donzalo's floor and here she was skulking through the halls without a stitch on her. Such a fool she had been! She should have given him the poison right off instead of that love potion.

Ah, well. There was a guardsman who had looked on her with desire earlier. He could do for tonight. And there would be other nights to deal with Donzalo Rosam.

~ ~ ~

"I do not like both of us leaving the place unattended so long."

"You worry too much, friend Blen. Do you think I bothered to keep a close watch on the staff while you were gone?" Jobareth took the reins from the soldier who had brought his horse. "It is but a couple of days. Enjoy yourself"

Jobareth Nafal knew that was a tall order for his companion. Blen was a man who lived for his work.

Both mounted and began the ride up to Castle Rosam. "Know you any Yule carols, Lector?" asked Blen of a sudden.

"Now that may be the most unexpected question you have ever asked me, Sir Blen." He gave it a moment's thought. "I suppose I've heard most of the old songs, though I don't know if I could sing through a one of them. And some of those that have been written for the stage in recent years. Why do you ask — if I might ask?"

"It's been a long time since I've celebrated the season with anyone. I was still a boy when I left my home to join the army."

"Well, I don't think the count will call on you to serenade him. For that matter," continued Jobareth, "I doubt they sing the same carols here as back in Sharsh."

Blen nodded. "I heard singing in the street last night in Old Laman."

"Did you understand any of it? I know you've tried to picked up some of the old tongue."

"Only a word or two. I'm not sure the singers themselves knew what the words meant." The knight looked upwards. "Fine weather for the Yuletide."

Jobareth gazed up as well. "Indeed it is, Blen."

~ ~ ~

"Do you have memories of last night?" asked the Lady Se.

"I remember being in the Lady Nosana's rooms and, um, having some wine and, um, leaving. I don't think I — felt well?" Donzalo thought about it. He sat, somewhat subdued and seemingly somewhat puzzled, by her side. "No, I did not feel well at all. But I don't remember getting back to my room. Yet I must have because I woke in my bed this morning."

"Is that all?" She looked knowingly toward her son, seated on the other side of the room.

"In the night I thought I awoke and a beautiful golden haired goddess visited me. What a dream that was! She sang to me and I felt like — like I did when I was little and my mother was alive." Donzalo suddenly gave forth a great sob. "It seemed so real!"

"There, there, my Donni." Se put an arm around the young man. So large, so brave, yet sometimes still very much a boy inside, she thought. "It was no dream."

"Come over here, Guesare. I want to tell this tale to both of you." The minstrel came to sit on the other side of his mother. They looked alike in many ways. Surely her curling hair, now turning gray, had been of that same gold when she was young. That laughing mouth of Guesare, his sturdy artistic hands that plucked both rebec and recurved bow so well — those were of his mother. But something of his fathers broad, serious brow and compact frame were there too.

"Many years ago, over thirty now, I was only a girl of the temple, not yet a priestess, much less High Priestess. It was a night of the full moon, a night of celebration, a night of abandon. The sort of night when women young and old might seek love where they will.

"I have told you, Guesare, that Jola's father was a god. He was not though he seemed as one to me that night, when the stars and moon sang a baby into me, there in the shadows of the hills. He was a young nobleman of Sharsh, traveling through these hills. Tall, he was, and very dark, and I could feel the power within him.

"I had never known such a man before. I have never known such since. But I learned that he turned to the dark ways after leaving me. Such a waste." She shook her head.

Lady Se looked at Donzalo. "You know who her father was." Then, turning to Guesare, "And I suppose you do as well, now."

The two men remained silent, Donzalo appearing thoughtful, digesting all this, Guesare seeming simply stunned.

"Donzalo," continued the High Priestess, "it was Jola who visited you last night. I believe she saved your life." She sighed, seemingly both weary and relieved to have told her secret. "She and Nosana have been rivals since birth. They were born on the same night." Guesare looked up at that, surprised.

"I never knew that, Mother."

"Because I never told you. It was a night of celebration for me, a good birth, a healthy girl. Nosana's mother died in the birthing of her.

"And now, Donzalo, you must prepare for your vigil this night." The Lady Se, taking the young man's hand, continued in an even voice. "There may be strange things all about you, strange visions, strange voices. Do not mind them but hold to your vigil. Do not leave the temple and do not sleep.

"You have done well to choose Diba as your patroness and protector this night. I might call it destiny, though I would usually dismiss such claims as foolishness. My daughter Jola serves the Goddess Diba and, between the two of them, you should have all the protection you need."

8

Guesare was unusually subdued and Donzalo was not willing to intrude. The two walked quietly along the narrow dirt path; ahead of them was a small stone building.

"You don't have to do this," the minstrel said at last. "You can be knighted anytime. Your father could do it when we return, or your uncle."

They stood now at the entrance to the temple of Diba. It lay within eyesight of the keep, which rose behind them, the last light of sunset gleaming on its highest turrets. The two placed their burdens on the ground beside them — Donzalo's weapons and raiment for the morning, among them a new sword for his knighting.

Though it was not truly new, but one with which Mausare had gifted him, one he said only had once been given him. At the moment, the young man wore a simple white tunic.

"It needs to be now," stated Donzalo, with far more certainty than his companion felt. "As your mother said, it is destiny. Or did she say it wasn't destiny? The Lady Se can be confusing." He looked the shrine over. "It's pretty small, isn't it? You should do better by your goddesses!"

"Diba is a rather minor goddess here in the Cuddon. Her father Jov and mother Esefa get the big temples." Guesare went to the altar and lit the oil lamp that stood before it. It's light flickered on the close walls and the small alabaster statue of the goddess, standing with her bow over her shoulder and a wolf at her heel.

He looked at his young friend and then embraced him fiercely. "Be safe and well, my boy. I can not wait here inside with you. I would have kept watch outside but Mother says that is not at all a good idea tonight — anyone out here is likely to be torn to pieces. So stay inside!

"I will watch from the keep. And, yes, I shall say a prayer to Diba."

~ ~ ~

It was good to have a fighting man around the place, thought the innkeeper, in case of trouble. This one kept to himself, mostly, didn't bother the occasional traveler — they were few at this time of the year — and rarely complained. Oh, maybe he drank a bit too heavily at times but he was a quiet drunk.

"Need you anything, Sir Perdos?" he asked as the man entered his taproom.

The soldier shook his head. "I'm going to go out a while. I need to stretch my legs."

"Do not take too long. The wife is preparing a Yule-eve feast and we would gladly share it with you."

Perdos gave him a long, expressionless look, almost as if he did not understand the man's meaning. "Very well," he said at last. "I thank you." He stepped out into the cool, late-afternoon air.

The knight was finding he liked this small village on the river. It lay well south of Ros-town, outside of Rosam holdings altogether, so that was of no concern to him. A few houses, a landing, the little inn — that was all there was to the place. One of the lesser counts of Lama ruled around here, and with a light touch.

He strolled for a while, the wide flow to his left. There was no traffic on the river, only bits of flotsam slowly making their way down to Morparas. How many leagues up the Weldar was his home? It had been a very long time since Perdos had seen it, or his mother. Did she still live? It was just as well that he didn't know and would never see her again. He wouldn't want to tell her that her other son was dead.

Ah, poor Percos. Always a fighter and it had been his undoing. He remembered how the young scrapper had stood up to their father, when he could no longer stand to see him beat Mother. That was when the two of them had to take to the road and seek their fortunes elsewhere.

One thing he knew for sure was that Dad wasn't alive. He spat and turned back to his lodgings.

So, what fortunes had they found? Death in an unmarked grave for his brother, outlawry for him. Perdos was tired of his life but he had vowed revenge on the minstrel Guesare. Maybe when that was over —

He stood a minute or two outside the inn door. He could hear the innkeeper and his wife bustling about inside, singing snatches of Yuletide song to each other. Why not? he thought to himself and went in to greet them.

~ ~ ~

Once, he thought he saw women in the darkness. Some danced. Some stood like statues. He wasn't sure, but one or two might have flown. Could they have? Some were naked and others wrapped in long cloaks.

Then there was a howling of wolves. That is a good thing, thought Donzalo. They are sacred to Diba. Perhaps her pack is out hunting demons. He smiled at that. To him, Diba and her pack was a child-hood story.

Right then, though, he silently vowed that he would never again hunt a wolf.

None of it seemed real. That doesn't matter, he told himself. Real or not, he had been told to stay put and stay alert and that was what he would do.

Then more women. Some, he felt, were being rather lewd. Donzalo had had quite enough of that sort of thing the previous night so he paid them little heed. Oh, and was that — well, it might or might not have been Nosana. The figure disappeared into a veiled crowd.

Only to come out carrying the butchered body of a young man. For a moment, it seemed to wear his own face, and to cry out to him for succor. The women cast off their robes to attack the carcass with tooth and talon. One looked up, directly at him, and laughed sound-lessly. Blood and entrails dripped from her mouth.

They are not in the temple with me, Donzalo told himself. Diba wouldn't allow that. Or Jola wouldn't. He remembered his golden woman, his dream woman, and fixed his thoughts on her. She would keep him safe.

43

~ ~ ~

Guesare stood before a high tower window, keeping watch. Once, he thought he saw lights flicker near the shrine of Diba but he was uncertain. After a time, his father came and stood silently beside him.

At last, the older man spoke. "There are things going on, aren't there? Things I don't know about."

"Yes, Father. But you —" He stopped.

"Go on, my son."

"You never wanted to hear of the misdeeds of your children. You called them mere family squabbles."

"They usually were, Guesare," responded the thane. "I know some of my offspring have done wrong. Great wrong. I know that Nosana probably murdered her husband."

"And almost killed Donzalo," said Lady Se, who had come up quietly to stand with them. "Jola found this in the robe she left behind in his room." She held out a small vial of purplish liquid. "I know this poison. It kills quickly but very painfully."

"She was in his room, eh? Well, I know she visits many men's rooms. That, I overlook." Vantare took the vial from his wife's hand. "But this —" He shook his head. "Ah, Nosana.

"What am I to do, wife? I think the girl has been cursed since the day of her birth."

"Do, nothing, my husband. We must watch and be ready, for more is certain to come and it is well we know who will bring it." She turned to peer from the window, drawing a soft red cloak close about her. "Our young Donzalo is being tested," said Se. "So far, he has proven worthy. I pray to the Great Mother that he will be found so tonight."

~ ~ ~

Wake up! He hadn't fallen asleep, had he? It was that music, that monotonous, continuous music. It was putting him into a daze. What wouldn't he give for a few more wolf howls!

And the mists. Now, he missed those lewd women and their contortions. These constant swirling clouds about him would drive him mad. As, no doubt, they were intended to do. Just when he thought he saw a figure taking form, moving through them, it would disappear again.

"Stay firm, Donzalo," a voice whispered in his ear. He liked the voice. It was a voice he remembered. He knew she wasn't really there, an illusion like all else he had experienced this night, but he did not mind. How better to fight illusion than with illusion?

"Remember yourself, you who defeated the Rupa, you who slew the Dogs of Asak, and do not fear."

He decided to answer aloud. "I do not feel so brave, this night." He waited a moment, then continued. "I do not feel so brave, many nights. I am often tired and I am often afraid."

"That, too, is part of being a hero," came the answer. Was that the voice of his dream? It seemed so, yet somehow unalike. "You have stayed alive. Remain so!" There was a liquid, golden laugh. "And remember you are not alone."

"Who are you?" he cried. A wind was starting to blow, clearing the mists from around him.

"I am Diba. But I speak through my priestess Jola." The voice paused a moment. Then, again came laughter, rich, deep, yet fully feminine. "Be good to my Jola. I think she likes thee."

There came a howling as of many wolves or perhaps it was only the winds, swirling through the shrine. Donzalo saw a faint light finding its way through the high windows. He went to the door. Yes, there was a rosy dawn spreading across the Cuddonian hills.

The golden-haired woman of his seeming dream stood outside the door. "You should be safe now, brave Donzalo. The new year is come."

9

The Yule is a time of cheer. It is a time, as well, to leave behind the past, to greet the promises of a new year. For Donzalo Rosam, the dawn of the Yule brought him before Vantare, Thane of Drolwym.

Guesare had come at dawn to escort him back to the keep, evincing little surprise at seeing his sister waiting with the young Laman. He had learned to be surprised by nothing Jola did. While he helped Guesare into his knightly raiment, she slipped away, not to be seen again that day.

Into the Great Hall in Keep Drolwym they strode. It was not that great a hall, really, and one of several scattered through that haphazard edifice, but it was so designated. There awaited the thane, the Lady Se, family, friends, kitchen maids, stable boys — pretty much anyone in the castle who cared to come. And since it was a holiday, that meant almost everyone.

The minstrel did note the absence of his other sister, Nosana. She had probably been up all night casting spells to counter those of Jola. Guesare did not doubt at all now that the woman had become an ally of Lord Radal.

Lord Radal — well, what his mother had told him of their liaison was still sinking in. The one thing of which he was sure was that he hated the man no less than before.

Donzalo went forward to stand before the thane, resplendent in white and gold. The young man was in white and gold, that is; the thane was wearing an old greenish kilt and an untucked shirt, but his wife had prevailed upon him to thrown an only slightly patched cloak on over them.

There was no kneeling here. That went against Cuddonian sensibilities. Following a brief recitation of vows, Donzalo handed his sword to Vantare, who had to reach up to tap the tall Laman on each shoulder with the blade, before handing it back. "I name thee knight," he said. "Sir Donzalo!"

The crowd didn't exactly roar but they applauded vigorously enough before going in search of their breakfasts. Some, it is to be suspected, even went back to bed, to rise later for this day of feasting and gifting and much drinking as the Yule log burned into the night.

~ ~ ~

Ansa, known to friends and theater-goers in the capital as Maresta and to some, elsewhere, as Posena, sat by herself on the day of the Yule. It came as no surprise to her that she was alone.

Fachalana would be at her father's house, no doubt, and probably at court later. She would have no time for her friend — friend only when she needed her, someone she permitted to address her familiarly but did not truly let into her circle. So, here she was in this empty theater. At least it was the best lodging she had ever had in Celatas.

Back in the Anian realm, her people didn't celebrate this day anyway. Oh, they marked the solstice with a religious observance but nothing more. But no one here knew she was truly Ani. They thought only that she played one on stage!

She found herself wandering about the building, wrapped in fur against the chill. Ansa had grown up wearing fur, on the high steppes. It would be good to see them again, to hug her spy-master brother and tell him she was done with this life.

And if she threw off this life, what couldn't she do? Where couldn't she go? There was one place she would like to go and it was not in the Anian Empire nor was the young man who lived there of her blood. She wondered where he was now, that tall Laman she had kissed once at Harvest Festival, before she fled into the night.

~ ~ ~

Nosana had made an appearance. It had been brief, and she had been surly and seemed very tired, but she took her place at the main table — she always assumed she belonged there and none was willing to tell her otherwise — where she picked at her high-heaped plate before pushing it aside and excusing herself.

"It is most unusual for Nosana to lose her appetite," whispered

Mausare to Lanta, his wife, "but it certainly improves mine to see her leave."

The woman, who appeared about half his size, did not disagree. "Don't throw your pudding, deary," she said to the little girl seated between them. Their other four children were spread along the table on either side.

The toddler squirmed and then held out her arms. "Unca Donni!" she squealed.

"Sir Donzalo can't hold you right now," said her father. "Let him eat in peace."

"It's all right, kinsman Mausare. Lift her over to me. Oh, never mind." The little girl had slipped under the table and was climbing into his lap. "Here you go, my darling." He pulled her on up so she could stare triumphantly across the board at her parents.

"Have you any children at home?" asked Lanta.

Donzalo lied. "No ma'am." How could he explain his past with the Lady Lomela and how it had gotten him into all his difficulties? "I've yet to take a wife."

She looked to her husband. "It wouldn't be hard to find him one."

"Indeed not, my dear," Mausare laughed. "A younger son such as you could do worse than to find an heiress here in the Cuddon," he told Donzalo. "You are not, um, like our brother Guesare, are you?" He glanced toward the minstrel, seated beside his mother at the head table.

"Don't be silly, Mausare," said Lanta. "Didn't you hear about him and Nosana?"

The Cuddonian's eyes widened some at that. "No, I do not gossip in the halls with all the wives of Drolwym."

"Your loss, husband mine. But," she added, "there are some parts to the story you might not like anyway."

Donzalo felt himself reddening as the two off-handedly discussed his misadventure. "In truth," Lanta said, turning back to the young Laman, "I am one of the priestesses of Rema. I heard most of the tale from the Lady Se."

48

"Then you probably know that I recall almost nothing of it," he answered.

"But you remember who saved you." She gave her husband a somewhat wary sidelong glance. "She may well have saved you again, last night, with the aid of our circle."

Mausare grasped her meaning. "You are speaking of Jola." His wife only nodded.

"That was long ago, my Lanta, so long that it seems no more than a dream now." He shook his head. "And I do not remember whether it was a good dream or a bad one — only that I awakened from it," he concluded, speaking as much to himself as to his companions.

"We will return to our farm on the morrow, Donzalo. It lies not far away; visit if you can."

~ ~ ~

"Copago." The count motioned for his master of arms to approach. "You needn't be here. Go home to your family."

"Are you certain, sir? They do not expect me this early."

"Then surprise them, and kiss your pretty wife and daughter for me. And —" Borrago appeared uncertain as to whether he should continue. "And wish your mother well."

"That I will, my lord." He looked squarely at this man whom he knew to be his father and spoke frankly. Copago ever spoke frankly, or not at all. "She always wishes well for you.

"And I wish the blessing of the Yule on you and all your family, sir." With a slight bow to his liege, he turned and strode from the hall.

As he went to take his place at the high table, Borrago smiled to himself at the thought of this solid, serious man in the little cottage he called home, outside the castle walls and all the turmoil of the keep, with his girl on his knee and his loving wife beside him.

And, yes, his mother there too, long a widow for the second time. She had been a couple years older than he, the widow of one of his father's officers. Count Ros has seen to it that she was quickly married again when he learned she was bearing Borrago's child.

49

Ros's own widow, the Lady Vibola, was not with them today. Borrago feared that his mother's time was drawing to an end. Most of her days she spent in her own chambers, huddled by the fire and listening to the old tales and songs she loved so much.

Would that Donzalo were here! He always seemed to bring cheer to his grandmother. But the Lady Lomela, aye, and her friend, the diplomat Nafal, visited often with the old woman. He should find time, too, while there was time.

He reached down to feed a scrap of venison to the pup that lolled at his feet. "You spoil that dog, Father," said Bolos, seated, as was customary, to his right. Bolos was drinking some hot, dark liquid brewed of herbs. He had not touched wine for months.

"Well, your boy isn't here to spoil at the moment." He looked beyond his son to the very obviously pregnant Lady Lomela. "Though soon he will have even more competition."

"I caught the young rascal trying to get at the berries on the garlands, this morning. If he'd gotten into them, you might have had one less grandson."

"Do not say such things, husband, even in jest!" exclaimed Lomela.

"My apologies, wife," Bolos said, briefly taking her hand to kiss it.

"He is standing?" asked the count.

"Yes, Lord Borrago," answered the princess. "And tottering about as well."

"Hmm. Donzalo was an early walker. I am afraid you, my boy," he said to Bolos, "would not get off your fat behind until you were over a year in age."

"And, these days, it seems my brother has taken to outstripping me again. Is there any more news of him, sir?"

"No, only the one letter that said he arrived safely in the Cuddon. It is best that no messengers go back and forth that might be followed."

"Oh." Bolos gazed out over the crowd of Yule feasters. "Yes, that makes sense. Who knows who might be a spy here." His eyes rested on the two Sharshites, seated close by. Not being an official ambassador, Jobareth had no place at the high table.

"I trust Nafal, husband," Lomela asserted in a low voice. "Of his companion, Blen, I am not so sure."

Both noblemen nodded in agreement. They, as well, were suspicious of Sir Blen, that quiet shadow of the young diplomat.

"Well, that is not something to worry about on this day," said Count Borrago, raising his goblet. "Let us drink to the fellowship of the season. And also," he added, "to the health of my newest knight, Sir Corgos. May his Yule bring him all that for which he wishes!"

10

"You are learning to speak Krevod passingly well."

"I've not much else to occupy my time around here," said Donzalo. "It seems to have much in common with the Old Sharshic I've seen in books."

"They speak that tongue still in some of the remote villages of Sharsh. And yes, it is similar to our speech here."

A group of children waylaid the pair at the bottom of the stairs. "Sing us a song, Uncle Guessy," demanded their apparent leader. The minstrel sat himself down on the steps above them and took out his rebec. "Hold this, will you?" he asked the largest boy, handing him the leather bag. The youngsters formed a circle on the floor in front of him.

"I fear I did not have time to write a proper ode for you, Donni," he told the young man, looking up to where he stood just above him. "But there is this —" He strummed the instrument and began.

Donzalo's deeds are all the talk,
I hear he did wondrous things;
He took old Asak's dogs for a walk
And clipped the Rupa's wings!

Donzalo's deeds are wise and just,
And widely sung by the bards;
They say he is a man to trust,
Who never cheats at cards!

"My brother cheats," interjected a small girl.
"No I don't," the boy in question objected.

Donzalo's deeds make maidens swoon
And villains shake with fear;
He often visits the man in the moon,
Just to bring the old fellow a beer!

That brought shrieks of laughter from his audience.

Donzalo's deeds are known by all,
The lowly and the well bred;
And maybe if he weren't so tall
He wouldn't bump his head!

One little boy jumped up and held his head, staggering about saying, "Ow! Ow!" In a few seconds, two others had joined him.

"Sorry about all that, Donni, it's just something I threw off for the little ones," said Guesare, turning again to his companion. He was surprised to see the young Laman seated on the stairs, his eyes misting.

"You've a marvelous home, Guesare," he said. "I don't know why you ever leave it."

"Neither do I, my friend. At least I have the sense to come back." He rose to his feet. "So what's to do today? If you get bored enough, you *will* want to leave Drolwym."

"I'd like to ride in the countryside. It's fine weather and I've seen nothing of your father's lands."

"That could be dangerous. We should see what the thane thinks. Or, what my mother thinks, I suppose I should say. She'll have a better idea of the risks."

"You think there are those here who seek my life," Donzalo stated.

"I do," answered Guesare. "There had to be a reason you were assailed during your vigil and Mother seemed to know it would happen. And then," he continued, "Nosana might have normally only tried to seduce you, not murder you as well. Though I suspect she would have enjoyed doing both."

"Ah, boy, I tried to bring you to a place of safety and I seem to have made matters worse."

"Then let us speak with your parents and see what is to be done. And I — I would like to see your sister Jola again too. Is she ever about?"

"Friend Donzalo, if you are to see Jola, it will be when she wishes."

~ ~ ~

Radal was impressed. "You made your way through all my wardings. Did you even know they were there?"

"Wardings, Father?" Fachalana was puzzled. "I — I picked a lock and found your hiding places. What else was there?"

"No one should have found those 'hiding places.' No one except a very skilled student of the art." He sighed. "I might have know you had talent." He shook his head and looked at his daughter. "But you've never shown it. Twenty and two years years you are, and never an inkling!

"Why, I could barely discern that anything had been disturbed." He gave her a stern look. "It's not the first time you've done this, either, is it?"

The dark-haired young woman shrank from her father's glare. "No, sir."

"So what do I do with you, my girl?" She noted that his tone now showed more amusement — and perhaps even a bit of approval — than anger. This is an opportunity, she thought to herself.

"Make me your apprentice!"

Lord Radal was surprised. Moreover, he seemed truly appalled by the idea. "No! I will not have you as damned as I am." He turned away from her. "Do not enter my study again. And never speak to me of studying the art!"

~ ~ ~

"My only wish is for a blizzard so that you might be snowed in here."

"You would wear me out, my love. I might not survive!" protested Corgos. "And then you would be a widow all over again."

"I was better off a widow than married to my first husband." Tiana raised herself on one elbow. "But I have a much better one now, so I'll try not to kill him. Well, maybe I'll try a little." She rolled atop her new spouse and kissed him. "I'm glad we didn't wait, even if you do have to return to Castle Rosam."

"Mmm. I'm certain, my dear, that Sir Paren suggested we marry now just to be sure I came back. As if I could resist your allure, wed or not."

"Well spoken, my captain! We'll make a courtier of you yet."

"I will be well content to serve as Paren's new master of arms."

"Ah, then that is the only reason you married me?" she chided.

"I fear I have ruined my new career as a courtier already. I may end up being no more than your kept man."

"Well, I'll keep you for a while, sir. Now let's see you *earn* your keep!"

~ ~ ~

"This fine weather can not last much longer," remarked Guesare. "Why, I've even glimpsed patches of blue sky over the past few days!"

"I had heard that one never sees the sun in the Cuddon," Donzalo said.

"These hills are not always gray." Around them lay the colorless, rolling countryside. A flock of crows skimmed the brushy ridge-line, to disappear into the distance. Their caws might still be heard minutes later, across the still morning air.

And there were sheep. Many sheep. This land was not so steep and inhospitable as the Lower Cuddon they had traversed a few weeks earlier.

"Mausare's stead lies not far in that direction." The minstrel pointed toward what Donzalo thought was the north-west. It was hard to get ones bearings here. "He ran off while still a youngster to be a mercenary and came back with enough wealth to buy a quite sizable place.

"And up ahead, some, are the temples of Jov and Esefa. They are the largest shrines for leagues around and the hill on which they stand is considered neutral ground," Guesare told him. "So it becomes a favored meeting place for our cantankerous clans. None would dare break truce there."

"Where is your mother's temple? Or, I should say, Rema's."

"We passed it already. It is no more than ancient stones standing on a hilltop."

Donzalo stood in his saddle and looked about. "Ah, that high spot back there? Then I truly am glad that I made my vigil elsewhere!"

"It would have been colder but, perhaps, just as safe. I — I consider Rema my patroness and protector." The minstrel seemed a bit embarrassed to admit to the rustic Cuddonian beneath his worldly exterior.

"He chose well, brother mine."

"Jola! How do you do that?" Guesare turned to his companion. "She is ever creeping up and taking me unawares." He scowled, albeit good-naturedly, at the woman who stood beside his steed. "I think it was her favorite game when we were children."

"But it was so easy. You were always engrossed with yourself, even then."

Donzalo bowed to her from the saddle. "My greetings to you, Lady Jola."

"A good morning to thee, my brave new knight." She whistled lowly and an unsaddled stallion, all dappled of gray, came up. Jola vaulted easily onto its back.

"I would ride with thee a way."

She straddled her mount, not riding side-saddle as did most noble-women, loose, unadorned white gown clinging to supple legs, her curling golden hair falling unbound to the small of her back.

For a few minutes, they traveled in silence, the siblings seeming to have nothing to say to each other, Donzalo unwilling to break in. Then Jola turned to her brother. "Mother finally spoke to thee of my sire."

"You knew?" asked Guesare.

"I have touched his mind from afar though he did not know it. Nor does he know I exist." Jola's voice remained steady, controlled. "It is a mind near-lost to darkness and despair. Only his great will has kept him from falling further.

56

"That is a brink on which I have stood myself."

"I know that, Sister. I have often feared for you."

"Yes, little brother, and I have known that." She turned, smiling, to Donzalo. "Near three years of age I have on him, yet Guesare has ever made himself my protector. He thought nothing of it to stand between me and his half-brothers, though they towered over him."

"It was more often my half-sisters. But they towered over me as well!"

The trio crossed over a ridge. Below them lay a farmhouse of good size, surrounded by a number of low, seemingly well-maintained outbuildings. Men and women could be seen working about the barns and sheep-pens. "Here is Mausare's cot. Do you wish to visit, Donzalo?"

Donzalo looked upon the scene with little interest, before turning his gaze to their companion.

"Go home, Brother," said Jola. "I shall tend to sweet Donzalo."

The minstrel looked into the dark, unwavering eyes of his sister and then to Donzalo. The younger man slowly nodded his assent. "Very well. I deem him safe in your protection. Safe *from* you, I am not so sure." And so saying, he turned and rode back toward Drolwym Keep.

11

Vanob recognized the two horses in the corral. Their owners had never showed up at their rendezvous. Could they be at this inn?

He'd best be cautious. They were the roughest of scoundrels and wouldn't hesitate to knife him if they felt it in their interest. The soldier slipped through the doorway and quickly looked about. "Perdos," he said.

The man he greeted glanced up from his tankard and put a hand to his sword. Vanob raised his own hands to show he meant no harm.

Perdos looked him over a moment and then waved him to the seat opposite his own. "Vanob, as I live. What brings you here?"

"The same as you, I would guess. Sojel disbanded our company and I'm at loose ends."

"Bring my guest some ale," Perdos called to the innkeeper.

"'Tis too late in the season for ale," the little man reminded him as he set a flagon down before Vanob. "But I've beer aplenty." He smiled at his new guest. "I have to keep telling him that."

"Aye, my own father brewed." He tasted of his beer as though it were a fine wine. "Pretty damned good, innkeeper."

"Thank you, sir. Will you be staying the night?"

Vanob looked slightly uncomfortable. "He is," said Perdos. "I'll foot the bill."

"That's good of you, friend," Vanob said, after their landlord walked away. "I've not had much profit lately. But you —" He wasn't sure he should continue but did anyway. "You seem to have found a couple of horses." He raised his eyebrows in an unspoken question.

"Yes, Van, I slew their owners and good riddance to them." He almost slammed his tankard down. "You and I, we're soldiers and there's good and bad that comes with that. But those two —" He shook his head. "Scum."

"Our comrades, none the less."

"I'd already left the company."

"Deserted, you mean."

Perdos disliked the accusation in this man's tone, though it was disguised as easy banter. "I owed them nothing. Nor Sojel. And not you."

"Very well, man. I was simply curious. It's naught to me." Vanob looked about him. His voice now became ingratiating. "So, a nice place. You staying the winter?" Perdos only nodded. "Maybe I could hang around here, too."

"As you will." The tall soldier rose to his feet. "I like to walk down by the river at this time of the day. Say, why don't you come with me and I'll show you the lay of the land. We can have some supper after."

"Sounds good," said Vanob. He smirked slightly as he followed his former comrade out the door. He might be able to milk this dummy all winter and then maybe even turn him in to Sojel when the company reformed in the spring. The sergeant would reward him, wouldn't he?

A half-hour later, Perdos returned. "It seems my friend won't be staying after all," he told the innkeeper. "But he, um, sold me his horse."

And the bargaining, the knight congratulated himself, had gone very well.

~ ~ ~

Nosana had discovered this cave, far below the keep, when still a small girl, hiding from her father's moods and anger. She knew the thane hated her, had cast her aside, given the love that was her right to his young wife and her detested step-sister, so beautiful, and she so ugly and fat.

And he blamed her for her mother's death. "She was only the first I killed," she whispered to herself.

She had found another to love her, here in the darkness. Nosana had not been sure he was real. She was still not certain. Asak, this presence had named itself, and showed her things of which she could never have dreamed on her own. Could she have?

All around her, here, stood her coven. These were real. She had brought them to this place, taught them, made them hers. She was as a goddess when among them, a tall great goddess who would destroy all before her.

Ah, but two nights agone they had failed. She had failed. Throughout the darkness of the darkest of all nights, they had surrounded the little temple of Diba, contending with those who would oppose them. If the young supplicant had stepped out, left his protection, however briefly, the coven would have had him, torn him apart in a frenzy of lust and madness. Within, he had the protection of the Huntress and that they could not breech.

She did not like having to send a messenger of the night to the great sorcerer who set her this task, telling him of her failure. Twice, now, though there had been no need to mention the humiliation of her first attempt to destroy Donzalo.

"Sisters!" She cried, her voice harsh, awash with all the consuming hatred she contained. "The great battle is to come. Prepare yourselves to conquer or to go into the endless dark!"

"The dark! The dark!" came their response and Nosana, for a moment, forgot the pain of life.

~ ~ ~

"I saw the two of you above my home, this morning," said Mausare, "and Jola."

"Is that why you are visiting the keep, so soon after you left?" asked his half-brother. The three men sat before a smoldering peat fire in one of the common rooms.

Mausare nodded. "My step-sister frightens me and I fear for you, Donzalo. Her flame burns too brightly and I was near consumed by it."

"So you were," said Guesare. "I remember, though I was still a boy." Donzalo said nothing, but only listened to the two.

"Ah, I was young, too, Guesare, and she even younger. Children, truly, yet she so wise and I so foolish."

"I wanted to put a knife into you."

The big Cuddonian laughed. "I sometimes wanted to put a knife into myself."

Donzalo spoke at last. "Children?" was his only question.

"Aye, Donzalo, we were children. I was, what, sixteen, Guesare? And your sister two years the younger — just become a woman."

"It was a hard time for her, Brother. I know that now and lay no blame on you."

"Yes, she was only awakening to herself. But now, she is full of power. And so beautiful —

"She is dangerous, Donzalo. She does not mean to be but she might take the both of you into madness."

Guesare spoke. "You are susceptible, my brother, to such madness. It is in you, as it is in our father." He leaned forward to warm his hands at the fire. "Our Donzalo is one of the most level-headed fellows I've ever come across.

"Still, boy," he said to the Laman, "be careful. Might I ask how you and the Lady Jola passed your day? You need not tell me if you have no wish."

"We rode," said Donzalo. "We rode and spoke of many things." He leaned back, and continued as if remembering a dream. "She showed me how beautiful this land of yours is, from its rocky bones to the ever-changing skies above. I think I could stay here, Guesare. I truly think I could."

~ ~ ~

"My father is actually encouraging my theatrical projects now."

"Trying to keep you out of trouble, my lady?" teased Maresta.

Fachalana turned and looked squarely at the actress. "Yes, exactly. I fear I shall no longer be able to access his papers, now that he has found me out." She gave a quite theatrical shrug, extending her arms with studied grace. Maresta was used to such dramatic gestures from her friend and patroness; indeed, she quite expected them.

"But the increase in my allowance somewhat makes up for that."

"Then we can repair the dressing rooms. My quarters are terribly drafty."

"Yes, yes, of course. It is cold in here, isn't it? I'll give you the money to take care of it." She shifted the conversation away from the boredom of business. "My Jobareth is undertaking to write a play for me."

So he's *her* Jobareth? Maresta wondered if he knew that. "That is excellent news. Will you take the lead?"

"I'm not sure. Do you think I could play Oemse?"

"Hmm, she died in the story, didn't she?"

"I can die quite well," sniffed Fachalana, before laughing. "I know, I would ham it up horribly. And she doesn't even get to use a sword. I wonder if I could prevail upon Jobo to rewrite that bit of history."

12

There was a cottage. It was a simple cottage, a little sod-roofed house nestled in a hollow of the hills. There, one afternoon, Jola brought Donzalo.

They had ridden together often, these past few days, knowing such a time would come. It was as though they stood upon a shore and watched a great wave loom on the horizon, knowing it would rise up, engulf them, sweep them away.

"From a distance I saw thee, that evening Guesare brought thee down to the great hall. I think I loved thee then," the priestess confessed to him. "And it frightened me, so I ran away."

"I, frighten you, my lady?"

"Not you, sweet Donni. Love has not turned out well for me. Nay, nor for those I might love."

That was when he had first kissed her, leaning over from his saddle. She was not loath to meet his lips with hers.

And in her candle-lit cottage, in her great soft down bed, they first made love and her golden hair fell all about her golden body and upon Donzalo. He forgot all other women but this one, this goddess-touched beauty. It was simple: he loved.

How greatly might a man love?

No more greatly than a woman. At last, in this young hero, barely more than a boy, the priestess had found forgetfulness as well, forgetfulness of all other men, of a world in which she had found no peace, of a life of endless longing. It had been as though she had sought long for a home that never was, remembered only in dreams, and had now returned.

She wept, but did not let Donzalo see.

Later, as they lay together in her bower, scented of smoke and of herbs and of the pines that called to the winds of night, the intricately carved roof beams dim above them, Jola sang to him a song, a lullaby.

THE SHADOW OF ASAK

What shadow does a shadow cast?
How long does forever last?
Where sleeps the wind before it blows?
Where is love when it goes?

If I passed beyond the sea,
would you wait and watch for me?
If I crossed the mountains high,
would you pray for wings to fly?

Who am I without my name?
Are the gods or we to blame?
Why must dreams fade with the dawn?
Where is love once it is gone?

If I passed beyond the sea,
would you wait and watch for me?
If I crossed the mountains high,
would you pray for wings to fly?

Could a man count every star?
Why are all things as they are?
Do you love me when you sleep?
Answer these or silence keep.

"I love you always, asleep and awake, alive, dead. As for the other questions — they do not matter."

"No, they do not, my love," Jola had answered in the darkness, and wrapped her arms about him as she drifted into sleep.

Why should he not stay in this land, stay with this woman, be Uncle Donni to all the children of the keep? he wondered, lying there beside her. She was not that much older than he — a decade was nothing.

Ah, but their differences went far beyond age. She was wise, wise beyond any woman he had ever known. Would he ever be more than a boy beside her?

Donazalo could answer that riddle no more than he could those Jola had sung to him. And perhaps, as with them, it did not matter.

~ ~ ~

Nosana watched for her opportunity. It would come.

Another message had arrived from the great sorcerer Radal. She liked to say the name — Radal. It made her feel as if he were here.

She sometimes thought of that powerful, far-away man when she took pleasure. What would it be like to have such a lover? To feel contempt neither for her partner nor for herself?

Perhaps when she destroyed the boy — yes, and her cursed step-sister as well — he might reward her. She shivered at the thought that she might go to him, know his touch.

His missive had been short and pointed. Wait, it said. There will be a moment of weakness and she must be prepared to attack, she and all her circle. And then — ah, then would darkness triumph!

~ ~ ~

"My old friend Corgos returned today."

"Oh? And how is married life treating him?" asked Mistress Sima.

"Very well, it seems. It was about time he settled down, Mother."

"Not all men are as domestic as you, my son." The younger woman who sat by the fire, stirring a kettle, snickered. Copago winked at her.

"I think my mother means I am stodgy."

"You needn't tell me that," responded his wife. "The whole keep thinks you're stodgy." She rose from her low stool and smoothed her apron. "Yet we love you anyway."

"Humph. I prefer to think of myself as dependable."

"That you are," said Sima, "and always have been." The two women looked at each other and nodded in agreement. They understood the man in their life.

Copago looked fondly from the one to the other, his mother,

slender almost to the point of being gaunt, his much rounder spouse, Janona. He was content to be here, to be with them and to serve his count — what else need a man?

Ah, the count. "Lord Borrago asked after you today. Again."

Mistress Sima smiled wanly. "Then give him my regards, boy. If he wants more, that is up to him."

Janona raised her eyebrows at her mother-in-law. Of course, she knew of her history with the count, that he was father to Copago, but Sima had never before shown interest in any renewal of their acquaintance.

"What can I say?" stated the older woman, shrugging. "Persistence pays."

~ ~ ~

"So, we shall send yet another envoy to Tod-ford, much good that it will do." Lareth tossed the sheaf of documents onto the floor beside his carven chair.

"As you will, my king. Better diplomats than troops — at least for now."

"Indeed," replied Lareth. "What of our other concern in Lama?"

"The boy is in the Cuddon, with his kin there."

"At Drolwym? You rode there once, didn't you, Radal?"

"Three decades ago, when your father had banished me. For a time, I rode many places." Some, not of this world, the mage remembered.

"He was certain you were a bad influence, even though your father had served him well."

"Yet remained a mercenary and an outsider until the day he fell in battle. I think, still, there are those here who think no differently of me." Radal gazed long into the blazing fire before them.

"Sharsh has been invaded too many times. The people fear all outsiders. Even," said the king, with the faintest of smiles, "those who were born here.

"Is there anything we can do about this Donzalo now? Is he beyond our reach?"

Radal turned to his king, the one man in the world he was willing to serve. "Not entirely, sire. We could try more assassins but at that distance they are even less likely to succeed than before. But I do have, ah, shall we say contacts at Drolwym. I fear that they be poor tools for the job." He thought of the pitiable woman who sent him messages from the Cuddon, at once obsequious and flirtatious. "Yet perhaps they might succeed where others have not.

"I wonder, though, if there is any point in all this. You know as well as I, Lareth, that prophecies, by their nature, can not be undone."

"I will not turn from my course, Radal. This threat will be destroyed if I have to ride into Lama myself at the head of my army."

~ ~ ~

"This changes things," Ansa wrote. "If F. no longer has access to her father's papers, she is of far less value to us. I wonder if there is any point in my remaining in Celatas.

"There is also the question of N. It is inevitable that he would see me and know me when he returns to the capital. From the looks he gave me when we met in Lama —" No, Ansa thought, don't mention the place. There was always the slight chance of interception and it did not do to name names. She blacked it out and continued. "— when we met before, I am sure he thought he already knew me from somewhere. I've no doubt he has seen me on the stage at some time."

Perhaps that was too much information, as well. Let's change that to "at the theater," she decided.

"Please tell me what I should do, my brother. Is it time I slip away from this role?"

She looked at the page before her and, for a moment, wondered if she might ask him for news about Donzalo. No, no, she told herself, she'd best not. The job was her concern now and when that was over, who knew?

Ansa would miss Celatas. She would miss the theater and she would even miss Fachalana.

"A," she signed and sealed the message, ready to hand off to the courier.

13

They were content. What more can one say, how better describe? For those few mid-winter weeks, Jola and Donzalo knew only each other, allowing the world beyond to go its way without them. But even love can not keep out the rest of life forever.

It began with a barking of dogs, distant, barely heard. Jola turned uneasily, sensing something amiss, a bad dream finding its way into her peaceful slumber. She felt Donzalo by her side and was comforted. Then the howling grew more loud and insistent, filling the dark night of a new moon.

The priestess sat up, instantly awake. "Donzalo!" She shook her young lover. "Awaken, Donzalo!"

He raised himself onto one elbow. "What is it, my love?"

"It is come. Prepare for the attack of darkness." Jola stood naked, facing the door, a long wand of silvery-white wood grasped firmly in her upraised hands. Silvery-white, too, was the light that slowly grew about her.

Donzalo leapt from the bed, taking up his long, heavy, straight blade, the sword with which he had been made knight. To his momentary surprise, he found that it was beginning to glow with that same silver light. There was no time to think about that now.

"Diba's people have warned us," said Jola. "Hear them all about us now!" The howling of wolves echoed through the night, yes, and the barking of every farm dog for a league around. "Whether they can aid us, I do not know.

"It will not do to be trapped here. Let us face them in the open." Donzalo stepped in front of her, sword ready, and passed first through the door. Jola smiled the briefest of smiles at his protectiveness — she should be the one protecting here.

The night was clear, the sky filled with the cold light of stars, the moon a darkened disk. A dusting of snow lay on the pines rising around them.

On an open rise stood cloaked figures and, in their middle, one taller who raised a heavy, twisted staff, a ghastly green light flickering about its shaft.

THE SHADOW OF ASAK

~ ~ ~

The lady Se awakened as well and knew the attack was upon them. Some of her circle were here in the keep, others scattered to their homes. All knew that this time would come and had kept watch.

She called to her serving girl. "Go, gather the others. The battle is begun!" The young woman, an attendant of Rema's temple herself, understood immediately and, wrapping herself in a gray cloak, hurried to fulfill her errand.

Se went quickly down the twisting stone corridor to her son's quarters, which lay near. She found him waiting and, with him, her husband.

The thane spoke. "They are being attacked, aren't they? Be not so surprised, wife, I do know what is going on about here at times." Vantare's voice became grave. "It is well that he has the Prince's sword."

"You recognized it?" asked Se.

"How could I not when he handed it to me at his knighting? It was wise of Mausare to give it to the boy.

"But he'll need more than one sword, won't he? Shall we gather men and ride, Guesare?"

Se shook her head. "You have no chance of breaking through the enchantments laid round them." To Guesare she said, "You, my son, might."

"Then I shall ride," said the minstrel and hastened away.

"And I shall follow, even if it be of no use."

As the thane went to assemble a troop, the lady made her way quickly to the castle gate. Many of her priestesses were gathered there already, silent and somber. "Should we go to the temple?" one asked.

"No," replied Se. "What we can do, we can do here. Follow me." She stepped out into the open field before the keep, doffing her garments as she went, so she might stand naked before the Great Mother.

The rest followed her and at cottages and farmhouses all about, women came forth to stand with them.

~ ~ ~

A cat as black as the blackest of hells, as black as night without stars or moon, its eyes a cold and insatiable green, seemed to tower behind Nosana, to somehow merge with her, to *be* her. Before her stood a great silver she-wolf, bristling in defense of Jola, but also rising from her. Each had been possessed by her goddess, each partook of the nature of one of these elemental forces that mortals named Diba the Archer or the Lady of the Dark Moon.

And if those goddesses existed on their own or were created and channeled by the powerful women who called upon them, even the wisest of sages can not truly say. Nor do the wisest believe it matters.

There were flesh-and-blood wolves there, as well, circling outside the enchanted arena in which the two sorceresses strove. And now, too, there were man-like figures slipping out of the darkness into the mage-light, standing, watching. Others, thought Donzalo. Which side are they on?

On the horizon, he spied a faint, ruddy light, akin to the glow of a welcoming hearth, and knew instinctively that it was the work of the Lady Se and her goddess. Did it bring more strength to his Jola? He prayed that it would, prayed to a goddess he did not know in a land where he was a stranger.

The members of the dark coven were keening, crouching, contorting themselves, and the same sickly light that had emanated from their leader began to rise all about them. Fantastical shapes seemed to overlay them, creatures of another realm. Donzalo remembered well his last encounter with such, his battle against the hounds of Asak.

From the corner of his eye, he saw a horseman riding hard toward them, dismounting and rushing to the edge of the enchanted circle, only to be stopped by its magic. Guesare, he realized, come to my aid once again. But maybe he can't help this time. He turned his gaze back to the enemies before him.

Now he saw that each cloaked woman was opening the way for a creature, as solid a being as had been those hounds, yet somehow the coven seemed also linked to the monsters that came forth. And what monsters! Some were as bloated cats that yowled with the voices of the damned and others hideous rat-like beings. There were slugs that might be snakes and things with wings that should never fly. Donzalo held his sword, this strange sword he had been given, and waited for them.

A slender pale man — no, not quite a man — came forth from the gloom to stand by Guesare's side. Together, they raised their hands and where the power of one had not been enough, two began to make an impact. Slowly, a glowing fissure, a narrow door, opened before the pair and they forced their way through.

"The witches have called forth their familiars," said the stranger, in a high lilting voice. He stood as tall as the Cuddonian but was very lean and lightly made. His skin was the color of snow. Both drew their swords, Guesare briefly cursing himself for not taking the time to prepare his pistols.

All the while, a battle that could be sensed more than seen was raging between Jola and Nosana. To those that watched, it seemed that the great wolf and panther were locked in combat, each trying to reach and rend the others throat and the women beneath them appeared nebulous, hardly there, yet they were the ones truly battling. Deep in their magical trances, they stood unseeing, all attention focused upon their opponent.

But the men did not have the time to watch, for the beasts were upon them. More properly, perhaps, they were attempting to get past them, to attack Jola where she stood battling in her magical trance. Donzalo, by himself, would never have succeeded against them.

Three armed warriors was another matter, yet still the results were far from assured. These creatures were not easy to kill and would try to dodge past the men, no matter how wounded, entrails dragging behind them, as they sought to reach the priestess of Diba. The men hacked and stabbed and Donzalo occasionally kicked and stomped effectively with his long legs, preventing their advance. Each time one was finally slain, its mistress could be seen to slump and fall on the hill where they stood, not dead but clearly shaken.

Your power was never enough, Jola told her enemy, *even when the moon is hidden.*

If my servants reach you, it will not matter, came Nosana's reply, in a voice as harsh and ugly as her true spirit. The two women had been slowly moving toward each other, a step at a time, barely aware of it in their trance state.

A huge black rat, it's back covered with oozing ulcers, leapt upon Guesare and bit him deeply on the shoulder before rolling off him, skewered. As the minstrel fell, some winged thing hopped over him and reached Jola before they could halt it.

Only for a moment did it reach her before Donzalo's long sword cut it asunder, but it was enough. Jola was hurt, with a gash on her calf. Jola was distracted in a battle that needed all her focused will.

It seemed as if the monstrous cat locked its jaws on the wolf's throat and shook her. Jola sagged, reeled, before catching herself. For a moment, the wolf broke free of its enemy. How long could she survive, now, wounded?

Guesare had regained his feet but he was sorely hurt, the blood running from the deep puncture to his right shoulder. He would not be able to wield a sword much longer but he took a long dagger into his left hand, ready to fight on.

"Use the sword, mortal brother," the stranger said to Donzalo. "Only it can prevail against yon sorceress now. I will stand here with Guesare." He paused to aim a blow at one of their assailants. "Go!"

Donzalo rushed forward, swinging his sword wildly, scattering the familiars as he tried to reach Nosana. He could not, for that great black shadow, that monstrous panther, reached down and nonchalantly batted him away with a paw like a battering ram.

So, it's real, thought the Laman. Then it can be hurt.

Indeed, the avatars had become increasingly solid as their combat progressed, the magical combat manifesting itself physically and the two inextricably linked. Now Nosana-cat had again taken Jola-wolf

73

by the throat and had her down. A desperate Donzalo, gathering all his strength, leapt upon the great beast's back, sword in hand, and stabbed deeply.

Maybe another sword would not have had the same effect. Maybe it would not have hurt a creature made of magic, a creature that was ultimately unreal. This sword that glowed with the silver light of Diba was another matter.

In a great convulsion, the panther threw him clear. Donzalo landed hard and was dazed but could see, above him, the two enemies, each locked on the others throat, neither willing to relinquish her grip. All around, the sorcerous wall that had enclosed them flickered, silver and green and flame and darkness contending.

And then it fell in a tumult of fire and the earth trembled. The familiars ran and were easily slain by the wolves who now rushed in and who hunted what remained of the coven over the hills until not one remained alive.

On the ground lay Donzalo as one dead. By him lay the two women.

Guesare and his companion approached them. "The boy is alive," said the Cuddonian, placing his hand on Donzalo's chest. "*She* is not." He looked toward the twisted corpse of Nosana.

The pale man held his ear close to Jola's heart. "She, too, is gone. Ah, Jola, how I loved thee!" He rose and took up the blade Donzalo had dropped.

"The sword has fulfilled its task," said the Prince. "I shall take it home now."

14

Lord Radal felt as if something had been ripped from him, a part of his soul he had not known existed.

And over the leagues, his mind suddenly sensed another that suffered the same anguish. It was a mind he remembered, that he knew, that he had touched and allowed to touch him. *Se*, he whispered.

Radal? She tried to hide herself from him but it was too late.

A daughter? We had a daughter? Ah, she was powerful!

Yes, and beautiful. I would not have had you corrupt her.

How? Through her eyes he saw all that had happened, saw his own minion destroy the shining, wonderful woman he and Se had created. Radal knew despair as never before.

And he saw Donzalo, and that it all hinged upon that cursed Laman. He broke their bond and walked swiftly to the library, where his daughter sat, practicing lines from some play. "Fachalana," he said, "come with me and learn."

~ ~ ~

"This land will no longer hold him," stated Se.

"No," agreed Guesare He stood by Donzalo's bed, his arm in a sling. "I could almost hate the lad right now, though I know none of this was his fault." He sighed. "I could hate myself for bringing him here."

"Sooner or later," said his mother, "Jola and her step-sister would have come to this. It was good that she found happiness first, even so briefly."

"Maybe brief happiness is the best kind," the minstrel mused, almost whispering, "before it fades."

"Anyway," he continued, attempting to sound less gloomy, "I'm glad he woke at last. He'll want to hear the news that came from his home."

"Do not think his mind is healed only because he awoke. It will take far longer to heal than those broken ribs he suffered. Or even," said Lady Se, "your mangled shoulder."

Guesare winced. He very much disliked being incapacitated, to be able to wield neither sword nor rebec.

"Many would not have survived such magic, so close. It will leave scars, albeit ones men can not see. And the death of his beloved will weigh heavily as well."

"I feared to tell him, but it was the first thing he asked. I think — I think he knew already the answer."

"He may have felt it in those last moments. As I did. That is a terrible thing." Se hung her head and wept for the first time since her daughter's death.

"I weep with you, my lady," came Donzalo's voice, low yet strong, from where he lay.

"And I," said Guesare simply.

~ ~ ~

In the hills had they laid her to rest, near the little cottage they had shared, so briefly. Donzalo stood by the grave of his beloved one morning, a morning when winter was making ready to give way to spring, and sang.

If I passed beyond the sea,
would you wait and watch for me?
If I crossed the mountains high,
would you pray for wings to fly?

OF DOORS: THE FOURTH TALE

1

"What became of my sword?" asked Donzalo, of a sudden.

"It's true owner took it back," Guesare told him. "It was only lent to us for a time."

"The Other who fought along side us?"

"Yes. It is his sword. He is a prince of the Fay."

Donzalo considered this and nodded. "I had heard it called the Prince's Sword. So now I know why." He turned to gaze out the window again and then down at the paper he held. "I might as well go home," he said.

Though usually a man with a ready word, Guesare was not certain how to respond. "You are welcome to stay here as long as you will. Forever, should you wish."

"One place seems as good as another," said the young Laman with a shrug. "Or as bad."

All the joy has gone out of him, thought the minstrel.

Donzalo held up the paper. "You have read this?"

"Indeed I have, young friend. You have a new niece. It is good to have family," he stated.

The younger man smiled, but only slightly. "Yet you keep running away from yours." Then he turned the conversation back to where it had begun. "Why did this prince give the sword to — to whom, Mausare?"

"It was given to Jola. He told her it was meant for he who would be her champion. So she gave it to Mausare, not knowing who else." Guesare realized that was the first time he had spoken his sister's name to Donazalo since her death. "She offered it to me, first, but I was not eager to take possession of a magical blade and all the obligations that seemed to hew to it."

He was silent for a moment. "It seems to have gone where it belonged."

"Jola must have told him to give it to me. She saw too much of our destiny." He spoke with a bitterness Guesare had never heard from him before. "I am sick of the demands of destiny. All I wanted was peace and to love her."

~ ~ ~

Jobareth lied. "She is as beautiful as her mother," he told Lomela. The red-faced baby squalled and he gingerly handed her back to her nurse.

The Lady Lomela laughed. "She looks more like her father when he used to have too much to drink!"

The young diplomat thought that an accurate description but, being a diplomat, did not say so. "I am sure she will grow in beauty while I am gone. Indeed," he said, "she may be toddling about the place by then and charming all the little boys."

"That long?"

"Yes, my lady." The Sharshite sighed. "I must go all the way to the capital and then who knows how long it will take to return? I fear Lord Doufan is not one to hurry, either in preparation or in travel."

Lomela pursed her lips in annoyance at her father's bureaucracy. "Surely by mid-summer?"

"As good a guess as any." Jobareth had been waiting for the nurse to leave with the little girl. Now he broached another subject. "I hear there is news from the Cuddon."

"A long letter, written by Guesare himself. Here, I'll let you read it." She went to a small writing desk, made of unadorned oak, and retrieved a sheaf of papers. "The count let me keep it here."

Jobareth sat and read for a while. Then he went back to the first page and skimmed through the narrative again before speaking. "My heart goes out to Donzalo. To lose so much —" He shook his head, almost in tears at the tale he had read. Diplomat he might be by profession, but the poet was ever beneath the surface of young Nafal.

Lomela recognized the emotions in her sentimental friend. She had wept herself on reading Guesare's missive.

"Someone will write back, I assume," said the diplomat, composing himself. "Will he be told of the Lady Vibola?"

"I think Donzalo is carrying enough with him right now. The news of his grandmother's death can wait until his return."

~ ~ ~

Perdos had come to like these people, though he knew the innkeeper would readily cheat him of his every penny. He had become comfortable here.

But spring was on the way and he must be on his, as well. Where to? Not far below this village lay a good-sized town where the River Tod joined the Weldar. That might be a good place to start, to catch up on news and rumors. Little of that had reached him here — most of what winter traffic there was on the river passed without stopping and the road and ferry brought few travelers.

"We will miss you, Sir Perdos," said the little innkeeper and his wife nodded in agreement. "You will always find welcome here."

"Aye, if I bring enough money. Or horses." The knight's gruffness could not conceal the affection he had come to feel for this couple.

"Horses are a good idea," agreed the innkeeper, "and we would never ask their origin." He winked at his wife.

Perdos laughed aloud. He had laughed more, these past two months, than he had in years. Maybe more than ever before in his life. "This would not be bad country to raise horses," he mused. "Maybe when I'm done with — with what I have to do, I'll come back and settle around here."

The pair shared a meaningful glance. They knew that Perdos had some unspoken quest that drove him.

What the innkeeper said then surprised both him and his wife. "We have no children, sir, and no heirs. If you wanted to buy into our inn, we would welcome you as a partner."

"Ha, you already have all my money!" Perdos mounted his steed, ready to set forth. "But it is a good offer and one I might think on. Farewell, now."

He turned his horse toward the river and the waiting ferry.

~ ~ ~

Every day, Donzalo rode to Jola's grave. He went nowhere else — the hills of the Cuddon no longer held any interest for him. Sometimes he saw her dappled gray horse running wild and the sight brought an odd mix of joy and pain to his heart, a heart that wanted to both remember and forget.

As he stood silently this morning, wrapped in the garment of thoughts he had woven for himself, a voice came, a lilting voice that he had heard but once, yet recognized. "I, too, miss her."

On a shadow-shrouded bench by the cottage, sat the Prince of the Fay, hardly to be seen in gray tunic and cloak. The eyes that regarded Donzalo from his white face were a misted pale indigo, the color of opals, beneath startlingly black brows.

"Come sit with me, Donzalo." The fay turned his gaze toward the overcast sky. "The sun does not love my people, even on days such as this."

The young knight took a seat beside him and looked out over the hills where so recently he had fought a great evil, both winning and losing, and then at his companion. A sword hung at the Other's hip, but the Laman could see it was shorter, lighter, than the one he had briefly possessed.

The prince noted his interest. "No, this is not the sword you wielded. It is not meant for one of my race nor do I think you will hold it again. The Moon Sword we name it. It is where it belongs now, until once more needed.

"Jola needed it. We knew that it would, in time, come to he who would be her champion. So it came to thee, young knight."

Donzalo considered, briefly, asking how the fay knew this. It doesn't matter, he told himself, and I've had enough of magic. He remained silent.

"She came broken to me," continued the prince, "little more than

80

a child. And I, I who am near immortal, loved her." There seemed a great weariness in his voice, the weariness of uncounted ages.

"There is healing in Fairie, Donzalo, and rest. You too may come to us, if you wish."

2

Grippo had become a rare visitor to his brother's home. The duties of an acolyte had increased as he neared the time of his ordination. Less than four months remained before he would be made priest, on the most holy of days for Kamatians, the summer solstice.

And now there was Borrago. He liked the count well enough, but his presence in the cottage made him uncomfortable. It could not help bring images of his own departed father to his mind, his light-hearted, often irresponsible sire who had wed Sima at the request of Borrago's father, yet had come to love her dearly.

Brother Grippo told himself that he should remember him in his prayers more often. Yes, and light a lamp for him, now and again.

He rapped lightly on the door. A year ago, he would have simply gone in.

Janona, his brother's wife, opened the door to him. "Come in, boy! Why are you standing out here?" Grippo remembered when his grave, serious brother had courted this cheerful, even effusive, woman, the daughter of peasants who had come to serve in the castle kitchens. Copago could maintain with a straight face that he had married her for her cooking but the acolyte knew that her laughter had really won his brother over.

Only the family occupied the little common room tonight. "Mother," he said, embracing and kissing Sima. He then knelt to hug his little niece, who was tugging on his robe.

"Why, what has happened to your doll, my little lady?" he asked, looking at the mangled and barely recognizable object she clutched.

"King. Bad dog!" the girl replied and then laughed.

Ah, Borrago's constant companion. The count had named him King, saying he was the only king that would ever enter Keep Rosam.

"She loves the hound," said Copago, speaking for the first time, from where he stretched in a chair by the fireplace. "She and her dolly were playing keep-away with it."

Grippo wondered just how many times the count had visited there but was unwilling to ask. Nor did he think it was his business — Copago would see to their mother's well-being. The young acolyte had relinquished any rights to have a voice in his family when he had first taken vows.

"There is a flagon of beer on the table," said Janona. "Help yourself before your brother drinks it all." The plump woman, of a sudden, threw her arms around him. "It's good to have you here. You must come more often!"

Yes, I must, thought Grippo. And, Kamat willing, may this always be my home.

~ ~ ~

"The Prince's name? I do not know," admitted Guesare. "The Others do not give out their names to mortals. Certainly never to me, though I do believe he told Jola his true name.

"Yet I have known him since I was a boy. It was he set me on the path to becoming a minstrel."

"Do you still sing that dirge he taught you?" asked Ourru, freshly returned to the keep. The big man lolled on a couch that was new to his quarters. Both Donzalo and Guesare were a bit uncomfortable with that piece of furniture, recognizing it as one that had formerly occupied Nosana's apartment. Ourru did not care and wondered if he could get his late sister's mirror home safely.

"There was a song he taught me, yes, when I was a boy. And others since, but I think I know the one you mean." Guesare picked up his rebec and strummed across the strings. He wrinkled his nose at the result.

"It was good of you, brother," he said with a wink, "to come all this way to hear me play."

"It is far?" asked Donzalo.

"No more than a day's ride," shrugged Ourru, "and that's not hurrying. I like to get away from the cot to visit here now and again."

"He was his mother's heir, being the eldest, and has quite a nice farm to go home to," said Guesare. He turned a tuning peg, strummed again, and nodded.

Then he began a plaintive, yearning tune, almost chanted, to the accompaniment of slow strumming.

83

Legends they tell, where the dwarfs dwell,
of fires that well from the hearths of Hell.
There chains of gold were forged of old,
to bind, to hold, in caverns cold,
where the dwarfs dwell, where the dwarfs dwell.

In secret mines a captive pines;
and the runic lines form mystic signs
to tell her tale. A whisper, a wail,
all voices fail — doomed and pale
a captive pines, a captive pines.

In caverns deep the hours creep;
to wake from sleep means but to weep,
caught in this spell. Does a distant bell
their passing tell? Within her cell,
the hours creep, the hours creep.

The clamor, hark, in caverns dark;
an anvil spark, a dwarf-smith, stark,
to his tasks settles, he casts, he fettles
his magic metals, the crystal kettles
in caverns dark, in caverns dark.

What fate befell, where the dwarfs dwell?
The hammer's knell would rise and swell
on the fetid air, a song of despair
for the captive fair, beyond all care
where the dwarfs dwell, where the dwarfs dwell.

"That really should be sung to a harp," said Guesare, almost apologetically. "And not with a sore shoulder."

Donzalo had been staring at the floor, seemingly deep in thought.

He raised his eyes to his companions now, and spoke. "I — am tempted to take this Prince's offer. To visit his fairie realm and see if it can bring me peace."

"Avoid the Perilous People," advised an earnest Ourru. "Peace can be found anywhere, if one gives it time."

Guesare slowly nodded. "Do not assume the Fay are good in any sense we know the word, Donzalo. They can be wise and kind, but also capricious and cruel. They will far too readily indulge their whims."

"Then they are not so unlike us, Cousin," replied Donzalo. "I am indeed tempted."

~ ~ ~

There was a tavern at Todmouth. Three taverns, to be exact, but only one that appears in our tale. We shouldn't even mention the one on the other side of the Weldar.

Todmouth lay on high ground to the north of, of course, the mouth of the River Tod. To the south, lay swamp. Across the Weldar was a smaller town, where goods from up the Tod could be unloaded for transport eastward. Doing so was rarely practical, which explains why the town was small.

In that tavern, named *The Truculent Troll*, Perdos sat and nursed a beer, listening as he could to the gossip about him. At a table nearby was a group of men, traveling traders by the look of them, and their leader seemingly a large black-bearded fellow. Perdos caught snatches of their conversation, talk of deals both good and bad, of towns and ports, and of beaches where smugglers might land.

He knew of such men and the business they did in the south, where there was much disputed land and little enforcement of law. Up the Tod lay Count Orgelo's keep and, by all accounts, that nobleman had more than a passing acquaintance with such smugglers, allowing them to bring goods through his lands for a cut of their profits.

This endeared him neither to the Sharshites across the mountains nor the Anians who controlled Morparas, down at the mouth of the Weldar.

I'll learn no more here, thought Perdos, as it grew late. Might as well find a bed and move on in the morning. As he rose to leave, the big man motioned him over.

"My friends are all deserting me," he rumbled, "or falling asleep." He waved a ham of a hand toward two fellows drowsing, heads on the table. "Join me for a while. Then, you won't have to listen from afar!" His deep laugh seemed ready and natural, but Perdos suspected the man was accustomed to acting a part.

"Maybe I can provide you with some news, as well," he said. "Otherwise, I think you might not have invited me over."

"Probably so, sir," came the trader's reply, "though I welcome the company, anyway. I am called Galaro." He extended his hand.

The Laman took it as he sat down on the pine slab bench. "Perdos is my name, a knight from the north."

"Perdos?" The large man seemed a bit taken aback. "Late of Keep Rosam?"

The knight nodded cautiously. Was this man an enemy he had made somewhere along the road?

"Then you are the one trying to kill my little brother!" Galaro exclaimed, and then held up his broad hand. "Fear not, I've no great love for Guesare and he is quite capable of taking care of himself. I will not, however, wish you luck."

Perdos leaned back and squinted at the man. "He killed my brother. What makes you think I won't try to do the same to his?"

"He might thank you for the favor. We truly hated each other when young. Now," he said with a shrug, "we go our own ways.

"Besides, all my men are here and they would not take kindly to you slaying me. Or I hope they wouldn't!" He motioned to the barkeep for more beer. "Let's drink to that, eh?"

"As good a reason as any," replied Perdos.

~ ~ ~

Lareth knew something had changed. His friend and councilor

had always been a reserved man, a man of secrets, but now Lord Radal seemed turned inward as never before, weighed down by some unspoken burden.

The king chose not to pry. It would do no good and there were other matters that needed his attention, and that of Radal as well.

"Borrago has grown cool toward us," stated the nobleman.

"Can we blame him? He certainly was able to deduce who was trying to assassinate his son."

"We might do better with his other son as count." Lord Radal spoke this flatly but his king caught the implications.

"It is not yet time to think of such things. We are still allies, officially, and he is a strong bulwark against Orgelo's ambitions." King Lareth rose from his plain high-backed chair and walked to the window. He thought he could catch a hint of the distant sea on this strong south-westerly wind, a wind that promised the coming of spring. "His heir, from all I've heard of my son-in-law, is weak."

"The easier we might control him, then. And if we could pin the deed on Orgelo, all the better." The courtier's voice remained matter-of-fact. "It would also mean less protection for the younger son."

"No, no, Radal." said Lareth, turning to his companion. "Let diplomacy have sway for now."

"Sometimes the best diplomacy comes on the blade of a sword."

"Ha, you quote my father to me!" The monarch looked at his old friend, so unchanged in most ways, tall, thin, his hair close-cropped, as always, and his beard shaven. Yet he was aging and new lines were etched into his dark, ascetic face.

"Let us speak of happier things. My son's wedding, for one — I trust the Lady Fachalana will attend." It was a royal command, rather than a question, but spoken as one friend to another.

"Of course, my liege."

"You have seemed to keep your daughter locked away, lately. She has scarcely been seen in society."

"She has been studying," Radal offered in explanation.

"Oh, a new role?"

"So to speak, my king."

~ ~ ~

There was a hill. It rose from the pine forest, but no tree grew upon it. Grass, withered at this season, covered its slopes and on the crest stood a great stone, stark against the gray sky of the Cuddon.

Donzalo sat his horse before the hill and thought. Did he do wrong to attack the cat-that-was-Nosana and set off a magical cataclysm? Did his actions at that nightmare battle lead to Jola's death?

And worse, had he ever any choice but to do so?

He urged his mount forward, slowly. It seemed skittish. Donzalo understood, feeling uneasy himself.

A door will open for you, the prince had told him.

And so it did, though if one did not look at it properly, it did not seem to be there at all. The young knight dismounted and led his steed on. A figure came forth to meet him; not the prince but another of his people, the same pale skin seeming all the more the color of new-fallen snow against his black armor.

"Welcome, Sir Donzalo. You may enter but your steed may not." He placed a white hand on the head of Donzalo's horse, which turned and trotted away. "It will return home on its own.

"Go forward, young knight, the prince awaits thee. I must stand guard here." Donzalo looked back at the way he had come. From this side, the gateway was large, bounded by stone pillars intricately carved with runic symbols, massive oaken doors drawn back. He gazed once more at the winter sky and turned to follow the passage into the hill.

3

In a small room, no more than a cell carved from the sandstone on which rested Mountain Keep, Sojel read his master's message. At last, he had received orders.

It was time to move east, though the Lord Radal himself must remain in the capital through the spring. Reform his troop and add to it if possible — there would be funds enough waiting for him in Oles — and do no more until further word reached him.

Sojel would have led his men into the heart of the Cuddon, had he been so ordered, but he would follow these instructions and wait.

Everything the soldier owned was in this room. It was all he needed, each item properly in its place and ready to hand. He began methodically to pack two worn leather saddlebags for his journey. It would be good to be on the move again, a leader of fighting men.

It would be good to ride with a sword at his hip and none to stop him from using it.

~ ~ ~

Blen shook his head. They were so slow!

He dismounted and walked to where the masons were taking yet another break. One of them made a laughing remark to the others in Old Laman, thinking he would not understand. Most of these were men from the countryside where that tongue was still sometimes spoken.

No point in letting them know I caught the meaning of that, the Sharshite told himself. It wasn't really an insult, anyway, just a mild jibe at his eagerness to keep construction moving. The 'impatient lover,' eh? He had to keep himself from smiling at the name.

Blen turned to thoughtfully appraise the rising foundations of the embassy. "It's going well," he said, evenly. "Fine work, men." That should befuddle them a bit, he thought.

"Thank you, sir," said the foreman, rising to his feet. "But it's damnably cold work."

"Better to get it done now, before the spring rains come," the knight reminded him. "It would be twice the job then." He looked over the site. "I see the rest of the stone has arrived."

The pinkish limestone blocks, much the same as those used in the walls of Castle Rosam, were stacked ready for use. They might come from the same quarry, thought Blen. I should find out where it is. Blen had a need to know things.

"Aye, sir. And we'd best get back to it." The man beckoned to his workers, who were decidedly loath to leave the comfort of their open fire.

Sir Blen smiled, knowing they would be back around it soon after he left. Oh well, the work was progressing, even if more slowly than he might prefer. He could have the carpenters in soon and walls and a roof would rise here. If Lord Doufan did not hurry too much, the place would be ready for him.

~ ~ ~

A tiny, hairless, naked woman came forward to take Donzalo's hand. "All we whom you call Others mourn the loss of your lady." The young Laman recognized her as a kobold. He had never seen a kobold but there were pictures in the books he had left behind him in Castle Rosam.

He had entered a great, cavernous hall. How could this fit inside the hill? wondered Donzalo. Stories said that such enchanted heights were but gateways to other worlds. It was not to be doubted that he had truly entered the realm of Fairie.

"We do indeed, my lady," spoke the prince, coming forward and bowing to the little goblin woman. "Sir Donzalo, this be a queen of the kobolds, come to offer her condolences.

"I welcome thee to my people's home." He turned to the kobold and exchanged a few words in a language the knight did not know. She looked up at Donzalo and nodded gravely in agreement.

"May your dreams bring all you seek, mortal knight," she said. "We shall help to watch over them." The kobold queen slipped away before he could respond, into the shadowed vastness of the cave.

"There was a great devotion to Jola among the little people," the prince told him, "the trolls, most particularly, but they are too shy to come here.

"Come, walk with me and I shall show thee what few humans have seen."

"Was that the language of the kobolds you spoke just then?" asked Donzalo.

"That it was. It is a serviceable tongue and one the People of the Sun could learn. Our language, the language of the Fay, has become exceedingly complex. Or languages, as we have many and use them as moved by need and mood."

"The People of the Sun — that is mortals such as I?"

The prince turned his pale eyes toward Donzalo. "Yes. Know that we only call your people mortal to forget that we, too, must die. To exist for millennia is nothing beside eternity.

"We — the fay, the kobolds, and our close kindred — are the People of the Air."

Donzalo told himself there must be peoples of earth and water as well, but did not question his host about it. There was too much else to see and learn here. Other fay moved about them now, some of whom looked on the knight with interest, others who did not seem to notice him at all, wrapped in what thoughts, what dreams, occupied their minds. They seemed careless of their modesty, apparently throwing on whatever clothing had caught their fancy or going quite nude.

All had the same snow-white color to them as the prince, but hair varied greatly. Donzalo suspected that some of the shades were the result of dye.

Great crystalline pillars joined ceiling and floor. Natural formations originally, the knight surmised, but artfully carved over uncounted years.

"You rule over all this, sir?" he asked his companion.

"No," replied the Prince of the Fay, "the Queen rules. I am but one of her consorts."

THE SHADOW OF ASAK

~ ~ ~

Before Jobareth Nafal rose the towers of Mountain Keep. One did not see them until almost upon the castle, hidden behind a spur of the Zadcelam. Above the fortress, one climbed to the pass into Sharsh.

The diplomat turned and looked behind him, toward the broad Laman plain, the river valley of the Weldar. One could see for leagues from here and further beyond, hidden in the blue mist of distance, lay County Rosam from which he had ridden.

"I'll welcome a bed, tonight," he remarked to his attendant, one of the soldiers that had accompanied Blen and himself to Lama the previous year.

"Yes, sir. Will we stay the one night only?"

"Most likely." Jobareth gave a thoughtful look to the young man, really no more than an overgrown boy. "I can pick up a new escort here if you would prefer to rest a couple days and head back to Ros-town. Or have you family in Sharsh you would like to see?" He wondered if Blen had given this lad any explicit orders.

The soldier seemed uncertain. "I've — no one back home, sir."

"But a sweetheart in Lama, no doubt." Why, the young fellow is blushing, noted the diplomat. "Then I shall let you get back to her embrace. But let us get up to the keep now, before it grows any colder."

They trotted forward. "I could use someone," Jobareth began, and then stopped to better organize the idea that had just come to him. "Yes, Pol, I could use someone to keep an eye on things back at the embassy while I am far away. Do you think you could do this?"

"Yes, Lector!" The boy's eagerness amused Nafal.

"Then we shall discuss it tonight, within yon walls. It is a long way to Celatas and it will be months before I can return to County Rosam with the ambassador. I will depend upon you, young sir, to keep me informed."

Jobareth Nafal smiled inwardly. What kind of diplomat did not employ a spy or two? It was time he had one.

4

Ansa held a letter from her brother, master of Anian spies. Use your discretion, as always, he told her, but it would be wise to leave Celatas.

It would indeed. Nor would Ansa mind putting putting the life of an agent behind her. Not at all.

The Lady Fachalana's friend, Jobareth, was on his way to the capital — the Jobareth who had seen her in Lama, who would know her for a spy. But Fachalana was the one reason she might remain.

Here she was, alone again in this theater. Ansa looked around the little dressing room she had reserved for her own use. Everything in it could be left behind and she could be on her way home in a matter of minutes, with nothing to tie up, no one to whom she had to say good bye.

Fachalana — she realized that she had come to think of her patroness as a friend and believed the lady felt the same toward her. Yes, she was self-centered and willful, but passionate and fiercely loyal as well. And Ansa was worried about her, for lately she seemed not the woman the Anian had come to know.

Jobareth Nafal was friend not only to Fachalana but to Donzalo. This she knew. Could she trust him with her secrets? Should she take the chance?

The decision must come soon.

~ ~ ~

"Dreams may be perilous here. Some never wake from them."

So said the Queen of the Fay to Donzalo. She sat upon a throne of obsidian and her long hair was as white as her skin. White, too, was the gown she wore, tied around with a ribbon of black silk. A wealth of diamonds was set in her diadem.

"Might dreams bring me peace, my lady?" asked the young knight.

"Peace, torment, life, death — who can say? We each make our own dreams. But you, I think," she said, appraising him with steady gray-green eyes, "have the strength in thee to dream what you will. Be sure to use it."

The queen turned to one of those around her and spoke in an odd, liquid language. The fay hurried away on whatever errand she had set him. Then she addressed Donzalo's companion in a quite different tongue, one of harsh music.

He answered in the same language and then spoke to the knight. "She asks if I have told thee one of my names. We rarely share them with your people.

"Jola was the only mortal to ever know my true, secret name. Be not offended, my friend, if I do not tell it to thee. You may call me Arsel. It is one name and it is mine."

"I am honored, Prince Arsel." Donzalo bowed to the fay.

The queen laughed at that, with a sound akin to the bubbling of water in mountain streams. "I have not heard you use that one in many years, my prince." To Donzalo she said, "The name means Wolf-friend in your language. Or something very like it."

The fay she had sent away a few moments earlier returned and gave his queen a slight bow. "I have ordered a chamber readied for our friend. He may rest there if he desires."

Prince Arsel bowed deeply and Donzalo felt it wise to imitate him, before following the fay from the throne room.

In the hall, he asked, "You are her husband?"

"One of three. It is more a ceremonial title than aught else, not that we haven't consummated it on a few occasions. Things do happen over a thousand years or two."

He who led them stopped and motioned toward a door, before turning and leaving without a word. "I think mortals make him uncomfortable," remarked the prince. "He, as most of my people, rarely leaves our realm.

"Here where there is neither night nor day, we lose track of the passage of our lives. That is why I choose to walk beneath the sky."

The room was simple but, as with much of what Donzalo had seen here, followed no rules on the shapes and angles of wall and ceiling. Or no rules he could discern, for the fay might see things with a different eye. It was comfortably furnished, even a bit opulently by puritanical Laman standards.

"I will have a meal brought to thee. Rest here a while," said the prince, "and we shall prepare for what comes."

~ ~ ~

Sir Jak sometimes missed the Bolos of old, the man who would buy a round for his retainers, aye, and drink it with them. With his sobriety, the young lord had also found a streak of the miserly within himself, not unlike his father.

As sergeant of Bolos's private guard, though, he could only approve of this more responsible master he served. A more cautious man he seemed, too, and at times a suspicious one, seeing plots where others did not.

Jak pushed back his hood to scratch at the top of his bald head. The night was mild and he did not need its warmth, only its concealment. He pulled it forward again, his face hidden in its shadow.

Keep an eye on my father, his master had told him. Bolos did not like his sire sneaking off to who-knew-where, unattended. Jak had quickly discovered that Count Borrago had one destination and one only, the cottage of his master of arms, Copago.

Had Jak, and Bolos as well, seen more clearly they would have bethought themselves of Mistress Sima's presence in that little house. But they saw only the count going off to conspire with his natural son. Between the competent master of arms on the one hand and his suddenly blossoming younger brother, Donzalo, on the other, Bolos felt his position threatened. He knew he had always been a disappointment to his father.

The burly guardsman yawned. Usually the count left Copago's cottage after an hour or two, but the time neared midnight and he had not appeared. Now the lights were being dimmed within.

Jak waited all that night.

~ ~ ~

A woman of the fay brought a tray to Donzalo. She stared at him for a few seconds and then, uninvited, sat herself down on his bed.

"You were Jola's love?" she asked.

The knight only nodded; it was not a subject he wished to discuss. He tasted one of the cakes she had set before him. There was a flavor of honey and some spice but, all-in-all, it seemed a bit bland.

The girl — woman? Who could tell with the ageless fay? — spoke on, with a little laugh. "I feared to bring thee such food as we might eat. The flavors we seek out in our need for novelty might well turn your stomach." She stood and came to where he sat in a low cushioned chair, all of purple and green silk. "These we bake to cleanse our palettes," the fay continued, picking up one of the little cakes.

"They are quite good, really,' replied Donzalo, and it was the truth, "but I could see becoming rapidly bored on such a diet."

She nibbled on the pastry she held. "Yes, they are good. I had forgotten how tasty they could be. So they become a new flavor for me!" The fay, whose hair was an improbable hue of red, looked down at him and smiled a smile, wistful and seeming to hold a deep sadness. "I had forgotten as well how tasty mortals might be. But you are not for me, young knight. Not now.

"The prince will be along soon to start thee upon a journey. Or perhaps not soon. Rest you until then." And so saying, she left.

~ ~ ~

"Guesare," came a voice at the minstrel's door. Framed there was a large, clean-shaven man in the garb of a soldier, a heavy sword hanging at his side.

"Habidros!" He practically bounded forward to embrace the man. "When did you return?"

Of all his half-brothers, Habidros was Guesare's favorite. He was the one who had been protective of him as a lad, when Galaro would torment him. Oh, Ourru was kind, but older and too often involved with other affairs to notice the bullying.

"I rode in late last night. They told me you were already abed." He shook his head at his brother. "You have the habits of an old man!"

"At times, I feel like one," said Guesare. "Have you breakfasted?"

"A meal awaits in the thane's rooms. Join us there and we can catch up." He turned and started toward their father's quarters, down the haphazard hallways of Drolwym Keep. Guesare quickly finished dressing and hurried after, not even taking time to comb his beard.

Both his mother and father waited in the antechamber where the thane usually conducted business, this morning the business being sausages and cakes and porridge with honey. Habidros had taken a seat across from them and was helping himself to generous servings. He had always gotten along well with his step-mother. And with food.

Guesare had suspected that the teen Habidros harbored something of a crush on the Lady Se. Perhaps that explained some of his protection. Don't be cynical, he told himself.

"I thought I was the one who sought adventure," the soldier said, between mouthfuls, "going off to fight the wars of the Siphic city-states. But it seems much has happened here of late."

"I told him the tale of our Donzalo last night," spoke Se. "I pray that the course he has chosen proves a wise one."

"Our kinsman seems a most capable young man," the thane opined. "We can only trust in him. Is there any more butter?"

"Here, Father," said Guesare, passing him a chipped crock. "Honey, too?" Vantare shook his head in reply, having already filled his mouth. "Well, Donzalo is capable, indeed, and quite level-headed. I am not sure those are the qualities one needs in the fairie realm."

Se nodded. "It a place more fit for poets and dreamers."

Vantare washed down his bread and butter with a gulp of cider and spoke. "There must be such a dreamer in him or he would not have loved your sister, nor she him." Se and Guesare nodded agreement to each other across the table. At times, the moody thane saw more than they realized.

"I hope to meet this level-headed dreamer," declared Habidros.

97

5

"If you wish, you may do no more than rest here for a while, enjoy our hospitality, and leave when you will. There are pleasures and diversions aplenty to be found in my realm." Tall and pale, the Queen of the Fay walked beside Donzalo. "I think you seek more."

"I — I know not what I seek, my lady."

"That is what you must learn here. Only then can you return to mortal lands to find it."

Arsel followed behind them, thinking his own thoughts, and speaking not.

"Once you pass through the doors of dream here, you may not turn aside. Destiny or death awaits." She stopped and met the young knight's eyes, thinking for a moment how their color was that of storms approaching over the hills. "Are you prepared for this?"

"Yes, my lady," averred Donzalo, "though I am not sure which I might prefer."

The queen slowly nodded. "This, I understand. I leave thee to our prince." She turned and disappeared down the crystalline hallway.

"Come," said the Prince Arsel, "and we shall begin." He led Donazalo a short way further down the passage and, drawing an intricate key from his robes, unlocked a door all of hammered silver, grown black with tarnish here and there.

"You may call this the Chamber of Dreams," said he. "It is as good a description as any, at least in your tongue."

"Did Jola sleep here?" asked the knight as they entered. The room was not large, or appeared so at first. After a few moments, Donzalo was not sure how far apart the oddly-slanted white walls stood.

"She did," replied the prince. "Sit before we make a start, Sir Donzalo, and hear my tale.

"It was some fifteen years ago, by your reckoning," he said, as Donzalo settled himself on the large bed central — or so it seemed at times — to the room. "In the hills of the Cuddon, where I sometimes wandered, too restless to remain in Fairie, came I upon a young woman, filled with great longing, great sadness, and very great power.

"And I could not help but love her. For fay and mortal to love is always perilous and more so for my people than for yours." Arsel shook his head and sighed deeply. "The People of the Sun fade away so soon.

"For some time, she seemed happy. As was I, who had seemed to feel nothing for centuries, but it was to last for no more than a few of your mortal seasons. There was that within Jola that needed more, to understand and to untangle the madness brought by her coming of age. She was both a woman and a being of great innate power, with none to guide her. Not I, not the Lady Se; we had neither the wisdom nor the strength.

"And so I brought her here to dream." The prince paused a while in thought. "Otherwise she might have been lost forever.

"Of what did she dream? She dreamed of the Huntress, I know, for she told me. She dreamed of her father; that she did not tell me but I surmised. The Sword of the Moon, too, was in her dream and so we gave it to her.

"Whatever she may have seen, she was no longer mine, after, but searched for the one she had dreamed. I see now that she dreamed thee and, aye, her death. Perhaps, it is not wise to know what one must seek, Donzalo. You may choose not to dream."

The knight responded simply, "I must, my lord."

"Very well," said Arsel. "You may see many things — no, you *will* see many things. You will be vulnerable to those who have power and knowledge of the arts, both dark and light. I will protect thee as I can and perhaps others, too, will be with thee."

The fay took up a cup of what seemed spiced mead.

"Drink of this, and sleep."

~ ~ ~

"The Chas is already at flood," observed one of Jobareth's traveling companions. They had just reached the banks of that great river, swollen by the rains and thaws of spring, turned red from the silt it carried.

Celatas lay nearly as far from Mountain Keep as did Castle Rosam, and the country was more rugged, yet he had made good time on the king's well-maintained roads. Much trade flowed through the pass guarded by that keep and it was increasing as winter faded. Assigned a young secretary of the diplomatic corps — a post he himself had filled not long ago — Jobareth had joined a caravan of merchants wending its way toward the Sharshite heartland.

Now the group was entering the northern end of the capital, where shops and inns had sprung up along the road in hopes of luring travelers on their way into the metropolis. At a distance, the diplomat could see the great bridge that Lareth had thrown up a few years earlier, the only one this far downriver.

"Flooded too, it seems, is the town," he answered. The way was crowded, bustling with travelers, vendors, soldiers, all about their business, and idlers with no apparent business at all.

"Here for the wedding," replied the merchant, "not that there wouldn't be crowds for the Spring Festival anyway."

Jobareth nodded, absentmindedly. The royal wedding — that would no doubt mean having to spend extra time in Celatas, as Doufan would be expected to attend. A year ago he would have welcomed the opportunity.

He reined in his steed. "I must part with you here, friends," said Nafal to his traveling companions. "May good fortune attend you." The secretary following, he turned toward the king's keep, high above the city, the farewells of the traders in his ears. He had enjoyed traveling with them, hearing their tales, sharing their wishes to be home again with loved ones.

King Lareth's castle was not his destination. Not yet. He stopped before an unassuming villa, the home of Lord Radal, set back from the wide cobblestone thoroughfare. One might not realize the house was there, among the many trees and flowering bushes, were not one looking for it. How many times had he passed through this little garden, just outside the tall double doors? There was the bench on which the Lady Fachalana had reposed, when last he spoke to her, before he was sent east.

Jobareth motioned his young aide toward it. "Wait for me here," he told him, and grasped the great bronze clapper.

He was admitted immediately.

~ ~ ~

"You may ride with us. Just promise not to try to kill my brother while I am around, for I would be bound to defend him."

"As far as I know, he is far off in your ancestral home," said Perdos to the large man busying himself with his steed nearby. "Well beyond my reach." He did not add 'for now.'

"Hmm, I did not know that," responded Galaro. "He will not stay. His wanderlust is as bad as mine.

"We travel north from here, keeping to this side of the river. There is a place," he confided, "a few leagues up from Ros-town where we can cross over quietly at night, and pay no taxes or fees."

"But perhaps a few bribes? I've seen how this sort of thing works from the opposite side of the road, so to speak." Perdos took a certain pride in the fact that he had never accepted such payoffs, not that he had ever been important enough.

"Oh, aye, that is ever a business expense in my line of work," the big Cuddonian admitted. "We may trade here and there along the way but intend to be at Ros-town for the Midsummer fair. You," he asked the Laman as he mounted up, "are not welcome there, are you?"

"No. But I intend to be elsewhere by then."

6

It seemed as though he were still in the room but it was, somehow, turned inside-out. Someone stood beside him. He sensed the presence but saw no one. Arsel, he thought to himself. Not really here with me but linked in some way.

There was a shifting, nebulous horizon. Silver light glowed in the distance, all around and above. Or did it come from below?

What do I seek here? he wondered. Over the course of the past year, Donzalo had grown increasingly confident, finding abilities within himself he had never known existed. That was all gone now, gone with Jola's death. What remained was self-doubt, a feeling that he had been only a child before, not seeing the world as it was, a world that held nothing for him.

All about him lay only the shimmering light and desolation. There was nothing here for him.

No, there, far away, an edifice of some sort. He felt himself moving toward it, swiftly, though he thought he had walked but a few steps. It was the temple of Diba where he had stood vigil, where Jola had been his protector and the goddess had spoken to him.

Did he hear the Huntress's golden laugh? How could he when there was no laughter within his own heart?

I shall go in, Donzalo decided, and watch as I did that night.

~ ~ ~

Fachalana could be infuriating. So apt a pupil at some times, so headstrong at others! Still, his lessons had gone well.

"Concentrate," urged Radal. "The other realms are always there but you must learn how to see them."

She was frustrated. Perhaps something to divert her mind for a moment would help.

"Let it go for now," he said to her. "Did you know your friend Nafal is back in the capital? He stopped here to report this afternoon."

"And didn't wait for me? Your diplomats should learn to be more diplomatic, Father!"

"He was in a hurry to see his family. Tell me, Fachalana, are you truly interested in that boy?" The Lord Radal had waited long for his daughter to wed and considered Jobareth Nafal a better choice than most. The fellow had promise.

The tall young woman shrugged. It was an elegant and dramatic shrug, the result of her dabbling in an acting career, and Radal recognized it as such.

"He is, well, a good sort, don't you think, Father?" She did not sound particularly enthusiastic.

"But not one to become passionate over, eh?" The councilor nodded in understanding. "You have known him all your life, Lana, and I think there would be no surprises there. He should rise high in the diplomatic service and with you at his side — who knows, he might even take my job!"

They laughed together over the thought but Fachalana knew that it might well be true.

"Let us try again. I will help you focus." Radal placed his long fingers, much the same color as the pecan-paneled walls about them, on his daughter's forehead. "Do you remember the words?" he asked.

She spoke the spell and he tried to help guide her thoughts. Suddenly, he sensed something else. Something that brought a knot of hatred into his heart.

He sensed Donzalo Rosam.

~ ~ ~

The knight stood before the temple doors, noting how they seemed of the same silver as those in the chamber in which he dreamed. Should I risk opening them? he now wondered. Would there be solace within or only more pain of remembrance?

The unseen companion at his side, the fay prince, offered no advice, only a reassuring presence.

Was there another here? He turned and saw a man taking form, a tall, black-robed man, and knew it was Lord Radal. Truly here but a phantom? Did it make any difference in the land of dream? He had been warned that it was dangerous to walk this place.

There seemed to be another figure behind, shadowed, but somehow linked. A woman. She seemed — Donzalo gasped. No, not his Jola but so like her.

The sorcerer seemed suddenly to realize this second presence had followed him, was sharing his vision. With a word, he broke their connection and the woman was gone.

Then Radal turned his attention on the young Laman, raising his staff and beginning an incantation.

Prince Arsel saw the man, knew the man, and attempted to enter more fully into Donzalo's dream. It was dangerous he was aware, every bit as dangerous to him as to the young knight. His physical appearance began to take shape at Donzalo's side.

He knew as well that he was no match for this sorcerer in the realms of magic. No fay had the powers of the most gifted among the People of the Sun.

Donzalo seemed unable to move. Or perhaps unwilling.

"You must choose to act," the prince told him, once he stood solid — if aught might be called solid here — beside the knight.

"Why?" replied Donzalo. The wizard's spell seemed to be further sapping the lad, already seeming too sick at heart to resist. The fay attempted to block Radal's power as well as he might, to add to Donzalo's strength and will what he could.

"For Jola," said Arsel.

"Jola," said Donzalo. "Ah, my Jola. To what realm have you flown?" He turned his stricken gaze to the prince and asked, "Shall I join her?"

"Not in the hell to which yon mage will send thee!"

A fire seemed to light behind Donzalo's eyes. "Then I must not go," he whispered, perhaps to himself, perhaps to his lost love, and turned to throw open the temple doors.

There before the altar of Diba, surrounded by near-blinding silver light, stood the Sword of the Moon, the sword he had wielded the night he lost Jola. The young knight did not hesitate to step forward and grasp its hilt. As he came forth from the temple, blade in hand, the howling of wolves filled the sky.

Radal seemed shaken and, lowering his staff, broke off the spell. But rather than withdraw, the sorcerer pulled forth his own blade, a blade that flickered with unearthly green light, defying Donzalo to strike at him.

And strike he did, the silver blade destroying Lord Radal's weapon as though it were the tinsel of a toy sword. The mage cursed Donzalo, his face contorted by spite, before his form dissolved into nothingness.

What hatred drives this mortal? wondered Arsel.

Before them now stood a great silver wolf and Donzalo knew that it was, in a sense, Jola and, also, Diba. The golden voice of the goddess spoke to him.

"Beloved Donzalo, I will always be with thee, but you must seek your destiny elsewhere and in others."

And then, for a moment, he saw the form of Jola, her golden hair falling about her, before she and all dream faded.

7

Donzalo awoke to find himself not in the Chamber of Dreams but in the room the fay had first given him.

"You slept long," said the Queen of the Fay, who sat at his bedside. "Our prince has told us some of what happened but I would hear the story as your eyes saw it.

"First, we shall allow thee to bathe and eat. Come to us when ready." She rose to leave, but turned again to speak as she stood at the door. "You were touched by the shadow of Asak, the great despair. We are surprised that you live. And," she added with a small smile, "pleased."

The same fay woman attended Donzalo as before and the looks she gave him seemed to combine curiosity and respect. She showed even more respect and some astonishment after the prodigious meal he consumed. Thrice, she had to return for more cakes.

Then she led him to the queen's chamber where Arsel and, judging by their crowns, the other two princes listened to the tale he told.

"The Sword of the Moon entered into your dream," stated the queen, when he was done.

Donzalo immediately answered, "The blade served its purpose. It should remain here."

She nodded. "We have another trinket to take forth with thee." The queen stepped forward and pinned a silver brooch to his cloak, in the shape of a wolf. "When our Prince Arsel told of the Diba-wolf in your dream, we had this made for thee."

"This shall be my emblem, ever more," said the knight.

"There is some small magic in it," Arsel told him. "It might help you find what you now seek."

And what do I seek? wondered Donzalo. Was that woman in my dream a part of my destiny?

He spoke. "Perhaps I know what I seek no more than before. What I do know is that it is worth seeking."

OF WEDDINGS: THE FIFTH TALE

1

A black cat lounged at the top of the stairs.

For a moment, and only a moment, Donzalo was taken aback, memories of a tragic night flooding into his mind. But this was no monster, only one of the many felines that roamed Castle Drolwym. He sat down there, on the top riser, and picked up the little creature.

"We might as well be friends," he told it, stroking its dark head. The cat showed no signs of disagreeing with the idea.

His friend Guesare ascended the stairs and took a seat beside him. He said nothing but was pleased with the change in the young knight. Donzalo had returned from Fairie no longer troubled by his great loss nor so wearied by his grief. It was not forgotten, of course; the minstrel realized that.

He realized as well that Donzalo had become a man and was no longer the boy he taken under his wing.

"I will miss your home," said Donzalo.

Guesare nodded. Nothing to keep you here anymore, he thought to himself. Not much to keep either of us. "We knew you would want to be traveling soon," he said aloud.

"Ah, Guesare, there is still a part of me that would like to stay. I think I have made peace with my memories and can again see what I loved about the Cuddon." He sighed. "Save for that one thing forever gone.

"Maybe I'll come back someday. We could be old men sitting together by the fire here, my friend. But my dream told me I have a destiny to find." He wondered for a moment if he should mention the woman he had briefly seen in his dream. Guesare might know who she was; the man was a spy, after all.

"Tell me," he began, "what you know of Lord Radal."

"I know very many things, Donni, and many of those quite unimportant."

"Well, does he have a wife?" Donzalo fervently hoped that the young woman was not married to the sorcerer, though he doubted it was so.

"His wife died many years ago. She was of a minor noble family in Sharsh." Guesare picked up the cat, which of a sudden had decided it preferred his lap. "I have heard that she was a beautiful woman and he was greatly devoted to her. If Radal has one virtue, it is his loyalty.

"They had a daughter, too, his only child." Guesare stopped. They knew now that there was another child, the Jola both had loved.

"Do you know her name?" Donzalo asked, as casually as possible. Too casually, no doubt, for the minstrel gave him a sharp look.

"I do not, but I hear she is an actress on the stage in Celatas, much to her father's chagrin."

~ ~ ~

Sojel sat in a tavern in Oles. He was not fond of the town. It was too tidy, too well policed by the smug burgess who ruled it.

Even the whores had to have licenses.

The man across the table was a banker. He was a big, hearty fellow, with a great soft gut, and Sojel was not fond of him either. He imagined himself spilling that gut onto the rush-covered floor.

"Are you certain, my man, that you wish to carry this sum with you? 'Twould be far safer in our vault."

Only by will power was Sojel able to keep himself from knifing the condescending fool. "It is needed elsewhere," was all he said.

"Very well. You will find it all there."

"But I'll count it anyway," the soldier growled in reply, and so did, taking his time. "Hmm, all right."

He looked up. The man was still there. "Need you something more?"

"Only to sign the receipt, sir." He slid the paper across the table to Sojel, who carefully made the letters of his name, and slid it back.

"Now let me drink in peace," he said. The banker hastened away, grateful to go back to his everyday business of bullying tradesmen and extorting widows.

On the morrow, Sojel would begin his journey south, down to the rendezvous point he had established when he had disbanded his troop in the autumn. Tonight, he might see about recruiting some of the fellows loitering about the place to increase their ranks. And then, maybe, pay the officially mandated price for a woman's company in Oles.

~ ~ ~

From her father's mood, Fachalana was sure that he had failed to harm the young Laman. Of that she was very glad.

And now she had seen him. Not really seen him, of course, but even her momentary glimpse in that dream world was something. Could it be a foretaste of a real meeting someday, maybe? He was most definitely handsome — despite that beard — and seemed troubled. She had seen the reason for that, too, in her father's unguarded mind before he broke their link.

Jola. She had had a sister and Donzalo had loved her.

Fachalana sat alone in the little garden by the front entry of her home, sorting through all the disjointed thoughts and memories that had flooded into her consciousness. Spring was coming and soon there would be flowers all about her here. There were many of the hibiscus her father loved or had once loved, the flowers he had planted for her mother years ago.

If Donzalo had loved Jola, could he not come to love her?

The thing, however, was to keep Father from killing him first.

~ ~ ~

"Your beard!" exclaimed Lanta.

"I approve," said Habidros, the only other clean-shaven man in the room.

Donzalo rubbed his strong, cleft chin. "If I'm headed back to

Lama, I might as well look like myself and not some wild Cuddonian come down from the hills!"

Most of his relatives gathered there for the Feast of Spring laughed. They tended to be proud of their people's reputation in other lands.

Thane Vantare rose at his place and offered a toast. "May both your journey and your destination be to your liking." He emptied his cup and continued, "And remember you are always welcome here, Kinsman, for a day or for a lifetime."

"Aye," added a young man — a teen-aged boy, truly — seated nearby, "that goes when I am thane, too." Then, thinking maybe that statement was a bit of a gaffe, he said, "Though I wish my uncle a long tenure!" This cousin, Casurru by name and heir to Drolwym, had come to idolize Donzalo, somewhat to the Laman's discomfort.

"I thank you, all of you," said he. There were many things for which he could have expressed his gratitude to this family but there was no point in enumerating them. Donzalo realized that he felt more at home here than back in Castle Rosam and wondered, for neither the first time nor the last, if he might not find all he sought right here.

Guesare waved him to a seat at his table. This was a smaller hall, one lying next to the kitchens, that served for more intimate gatherings. This night, it was crowded with kin come not only to celebrate the holiday but to bid their guest farewell.

"The equinox is a rather solemn feast in Lama," Donzalo said to the minstrel, "preceded by fasting. We would be going to bed hungry on this Spring Feast eve."

"You more than make up for it at your May Festival," replied Guesare. "We barely mark that day, though it is sacred to the goddess Esefa."

"Does your mother celebrate it?" Donzalo helped himself from the steaming platters and bowls. The fare was heavy on root vegetables at this time of year, before the first fruits of the season. That and the ubiquitous mutton of the Cuddonian diet.

"I assume she does. She disappears with her circle and Jov only knows what they get up to!

"You should reach home well before May Festival. I know not when I shall find my way again to County Rosam." Guesare offered him a bowl of mashed turnips, which the Laman declined, as politely as he was able.

"Make certain that shoulder is healed first. You need be able to wield a sword before you travel."

"It gets better but far too slowly. There is still some stiffness," admitted the minstrel. "At least, I can play the rebec as well as ever. Or as poorly," he laughed.

"My roads and yours must diverge for a while, anyway. In the mean time, I do trust my brother Habidros to keep you safe on your journey."

"I am grateful for his offer, though a bit puzzled by it," Donzalo said. "We have only just met."

"He was between wars," Guesare told him, "and Habidros becomes easily bored. It is a failing we share. He welcomed the chance to see new lands." The Cuddonian leaned in close. "I did promise him payment from my Anian allies. My brother is a mercenary, after all.

"Which is not to say that he is in any way not to be trusted. I think he would have gone without the offer of money." Mostly because my mother asked, he said to himself. "He likes you, too."

"Well, that is to the good. 'Twould be a weary journey, otherwise!"

2

At another table, westward beyond Lama, beyond the mountains, Jobareth Nafal ate with his own family. The large dining room, its tall, arched windows opening to a view of the capital city below, only hinted of the family's wealth. It would not do to flaunt it and rouse the jealousy of the old nobility.

"I need to take some of this back with me," he said, swirling the wine in his goblet.

"You've come to the right place for it, my boy," replied his father, to laughter up and down the board. The Nafals knew wine, traded in wine, lived wine.

"Is the wine so bad in Lama?" his mother asked.

"Yes," said one of his older brothers, "how is the wine there?"

"I once had a white from the south I thought rather decent," broke in another.

"Mediocre, for the most part," opined the young diplomat. "Not particularly bad, not particularly good."

The elder Nafal considered that for a moment, absently stroking his neat pointed beard. "There's money to be made in mediocrity. Cheap but decent wine would find a market, if only it could be transported here more readily," said he.

Jobareth nodded his agreement. "If the southern passes were safer, it might be. But that is a job for the king and for my master."

"Then you must speak to Lord Radal about it as soon as possible," joked one of the brothers. "We shall hold you personally responsible for getting it done."

The young man had seen the Lord Radal again the previous day. He seemed haggard, worn, as if he had just come from some grueling contest. Their brief conversation was primarily of Lord Doufan. That nobleman seemed interested only in the royal wedding and not in the particulars of his upcoming ambassadorship.

"My master, as a rule, does not ask my advice," he dryly told his family.

"Then work on the daughter," suggested his mother, with an oh-so-innocent smile. She wants to play match-maker, thought Jobareth. It would be a good match, of course — for everyone but the couple.

He fell into banter, rather than acknowledge her implications. "That might prove a more difficult undertaking than the father." There were chuckles all around the table; they well knew the Lady Fachalana.

The royal wedding would be on the morrow, the equinox, the Feast of Spring. Maybe they could get down to business when that was done. In the mean time, Jobareth could enjoy this visit with his family, take in the theater.

Twice, he had missed Fachalana at her father's home but she had sent him an invitation to the premiere production at her theater. That, he did not intend to miss.

~ ~ ~

Count Borrago's renewed relationship with the widow Sima had become an open secret. Most thought it a most wonderful and interesting secret and readily shared it with their friends.

Lord Bolos was not inclined to agree. "My father is making a fool of himself," he told the hierophant, "and dishonoring the memory of my mother."

The high priest did not choose to mention that Bolos himself had never seen anything wrong with chasing after every woman who passed his way. But that was not really the same thing as this liaison.

He did, however, disconcert Borrago's heir further by letting him know that the count had spoken privately to him of marriage.

This served only to make Bolos the more suspicious of his half-brother. He had never had anything against Copago but neither had he ever much liked him. He would not have long remained master of arms were Bolos to become count.

But if Borrago were to marry Sima! Would Copago be legitimized? He would then be the oldest brother and could lay claim to Bolos's inheritance.

The king in Sharsh, father of his wife, grandfather of his own heir, would never permit that to happen. This Bolos knew for certain; all else remained far too uncertain.

At times like this, Bolos very much wanted a drink.

~ ~ ~

"Modareth and Carrana, in this year, the Twenty-ninth in the reign of Lareth, the One thousand, Three hundred, and Twenty-first since the Great Devastation, shall be legally joined in marriage." The Chief Scribe of Sharsh placed the marriage contract before them on his portable desk. "Sign your names, please."

They so did and the old man witnessed their signatures, before holding the paper up to the applause of the crowd.

At that point, the High Priest of Jov stepped forward to give his blessing. This, of course, was what everyone wanted to see, as it was far more theatrical than the signing of a legal document.

Prince Modareth drew himself up to his full height, which was not much. His shock of unruly black hair rose above him like a rooster's comb, surmounting a head that seemed too large for its body.

Scrawny, his brother called him but no one else dared.

The priest took the bride's hand and placed it in the groom's. To himself, he thought that it should be other way around. The Lady Carrana certainly out-sized her new husband in almost every respect, not that that was difficult.

"I shall be Modareth, at one with my husband," vowed Carrana.

"And I shall be Carrana, as one with my wife," responded Modareth.

"Then so shall it be and the blessings of the gods be on you," spoke the priest. He was pleased to see what seemed real affection between the two as Modareth kissed his bride. Two misfits, he thought, despite their noble blood. It's good that they have found each other.

King Lareth was pleased as well. Two wives had he buried and had loved each, in his way, but they had been political matches. Not that there was anything wrong with the politics here, but it was good to see his younger son happy.

If only the older one might be!

That older son, Prince Gawis, and he joined the procession behind the newlyweds, following them to the wedding feast. It was not that Gawis disliked the meek Mara, but his wife had given him only daughters.

Where is Mara? he wondered, looking into the crowd. Ah, there, with his three beloved granddaughters. Lareth did hope that his son would not make the mistake of putting her aside, once he was no longer there to forbid it. It would be unwise to divorce a daughter of the Partanacan emperor.

Dark the princess was, as dark as had been Radal's father, and, as royalty goes, a handsome woman. He waved toward them and saw Mara's smile as she bent to whisper to the girls. Telling them to wave to Grandfather, Lareth supposed. By then he had passed them and entered the great festively-striped pavilion erected for the wedding reception.

The king sighed. Politics would be the order for the rest of this day, a tedious afternoon of greetings and small talk with minor noblemen and functionaries. Duty called and Lareth, with forced smile, answered.

~ ~ ~

"Before you leave me for my brother, I ask one more service of you."

Count Borrago leaned forward, resting his elbows on his desk. Corgos's friend and commanding officer — Copago, the count's master of arms — stood gazing out the narrow window, seemingly uninterested in their conversation. Corgos knew better.

"One task or a hundred, my lord. I will serve as long as you desire."

Borrago glanced toward Copago and half-smiled. They had expected no less of the man.

"My son should soon be returning from the north. I know you

rode in those lands before you served me here." There seemed to be a question implied so the knight nodded his head.

"Yes, sir, I did." He had no desire to speak further of his years as a wandering mercenary.

"Then what I ask of you, Sir Corgos, is to ride north and fetch Donzalo home."

The master of arms turned to them. "We can readily spare a half-dozen men or so. More, I fear, would attract too much attention to you."

Corgos looked from the one man to the other. "All the way to the Cuddon?"

"Most likely not," said the count. "We have reason to believe he is already on his way or soon will be."

Copago sat down beside his friend. "He may need protection." He shook his head. "We know not by what route he will travel nor how many his companions might be. That, wisely, has been kept secret.

"If he returns as he went, through the Cuddon, there is naught we can do, but if he chooses to ride through Lama, you may meet him on the road."

"Or," added the count, "if you do not, then ride on to Drolwym and learn what you can."

"I should take the Great Road, then, my lord?" asked Corgos.

"Yes. A party of armed men skulking on the back ways would raise suspicion."

Copago nodded his agreement. "You will pose as a mercenary band heading to the Siphic cities. We will provide you with the proper papers. Count Borrago's name on a document has weight anywhere in Lama."

"I should hope so!" laughed the nobleman.

"If Donzalo chooses to travel by back roads, then you may pass each other unknowingly. So be it," continued Sir Copago. "We can do only what we can do."

3

"We will ride with you a while," said Mausare, "a day or two, perhaps." Guesare sat his pony beside his half-brother.

"Welcome you are, Brothers." Habidros had four men at arms with him, doughty veterans from his father's garrison. The Cuddon was not always a peaceful place.

With his brothers and Donzalo, that made eight men riding westward from Keep Drolwym.

Or mostly westward, though their way sometimes trended north and at times Donzalo felt sure they were headed back the way they came. Silently and in single file, they traversed the fog-shrouded hills, following barely visible sheep paths, passing secluded huts. Were there shepherds within, huddled about their peat fires?

In the mists, he thought once he caught a glimpse of a gray dappled horse, disappearing across the moors.

Habidros halted of a sudden and held up a gauntleted hand. "Brothers," said he, "here we must decide. Do we continue this north by west course or turn aside to meet the Great Road south of Oles?"

The others bunched around him. "Turn, I say. It is safer to take the back roads," was the opinion of Guesare.

"We would attract less suspicion if we come to Oles by the Siphic Road before turning south," said Habidros. "They are used to seeing armed strangers pass through."

The men-at-arms all nodded their heads in agreement with this. Being Cuddonians, they would not allow themselves to be left out of the discussion.

Mausare spoke. "Donzalo should decide. This is his journey."

"Aye, that's true," agreed Habidros. "What say you, lad?"

"Which way is the shorter?" asked the Laman.

"We could save a day's travel by turning now," Guesare said, "despite being the rougher road."

"Maybe two," said one of the men at arms.

"Then turn we shall. Though," sighed Donzalo, "I would greatly liked to have seen Oles."

"It wouldn't have been safe to enter the city, anyway," Mausare told him. There were murmurs of agreement from the others.

"There is a road over — that way, isn't there?" asked Habidros, pointing toward a ridge to the left of the trail they had been following.

"Of sorts," said Guesare. He looked to the sky. "I do believe this fog is going to lift soon."

"If we see the sun it must mean that we are leaving the Cuddon," Donzalo replied. "Let's get going."

~ ~ ~

"You must tell me all about the wedding!"

"Oh, I shall," said the Lady Fachalana, "but first we must decide what to do about Jobareth Nafal. He will be coming to our opening tonight and he will want to come backstage."

"Let him," answered Ansa. "He might as well know what we have been up to."

"Indeed?" Fachalana arched her dark eyebrows. "I thought I was the reckless one!"

"Better to make him a friend and co-conspirator now than to forever worry about him discovering who I am. I have been thinking on this for some time." It will also provide a cover for my other, true mission as a spy, Ansa told herself.

"Hmm, I do suppose there is no reason Jobo shouldn't know. He will wonder about our motivation."

"Tell him straight out that you have a crush on Donzalo and make him jealous." Ansa attempted to say this seriously but then giggled.

As did Fachalana. Then she sighed. "Ah, Jobareth will never be jealous over me. His heart belongs to his princess."

Ansa fully recognized that her friend and patron was being dramatic. It might be true that Nafal would always adore the Lady Lomela, but neither had Fachalana any real interest in winning the man's love. Even if it was entirely possible that they might end up married to each other.

"All is set for tonight's performance," she said aloud. "Let us go to my dressing room and share some wine while you fill me in on every detail of the royal wedding. What did the bride wear? What did *you* wear?"

~ ~ ~

The Great Road paralleled the River Weldar, here closer, here winding into the countryside and through village and manor. From Morparas to Oles it ran and from there one might turn east toward the valley of the Siph or west to Mountain Keep and the mountained borders of Sharsh.

In the days of Anian rule had it been built, so men and materials might move efficiently east of the Weldar. There were other roads, on both sides of the river, but this was, indeed, the greatest of them, kept open and maintained by the noblemen though whose lands it passed. None would dare close it to traffic, any more than they would the river itself.

As Donzalo and his party threaded their way down from the Cuddonian hills to find the highway and, further south, Sir Corgos prepared to ride toward them, others followed lesser roads along the western banks of the Weldar.

Far to the north, Sojel led forth the handful of men he had recruited in Oles. A pitiful bunch, he felt, but probably no worse than the usual riff-raff — as good as those who were to gather at their rendezvous point, anyway. He hoped Vanob would show up and help him whip these dregs into something resembling fighting men.

~ ~ ~

Neither king nor crown prince attended that night, but the royal newlyweds were in the audience. The bookish, retiring Modareth had never been known as a patron of the theater. It seemed his new wife intended to change that. Together they sat in their box, the prince nervously surveying the crowd. He did not much like being in public.

He toyed with the reading glass he always wore hung around his neck and turned to look fondly upon his spouse. She was no beauty, he knew, plump and large of bone, but he knew also that she adored him. Why, he truly did not know.

But Modareth accepted it and, so, chose to adore her as well.

There was a small window opening above the stage where one might look out upon the house. Ansa and Fachalana were doing just that.

"There is Nafal, front and center," said Ansa, "as you expected."

"Jobareth does love the theater, Maresta," answered Fachalana, for she still knew the Anian by that name. "I hope he enjoys this old warhorse we chose to present."

"It is a classic, my lady."

"So you keep telling me. I am glad our royal couple came. I've known Modareth since he was a toddler. Ha, I guess I was a toddler as well!"

"You are of an age?"

"Yes, as is Jobo. He somewhat took Modi under his wing when he first came to court." She sighed and Ansa sensed the true emotion behind it. "The three of us were inseparable for a time. We and," she added, "little Lomela when she came along."

The actress chose not to press further in that particular direction. "Did you know the Lady Carrana?"

Fachalana turned from their portal. "Not well. I probably treated her badly. She always seemed too — needy, I might say. Too eager to please.

"But she pleases Modareth and I am glad of that. Love is not to be cast aside, wherever we may find it."

Both women silently nodded agreement to that. And each pictured the same tall Laman in her mind.

4

"You should be able to pick up the Great Road by mid-morn tomorrow." Guesare stirred the campfire before him. "We will head back home at dawn."

Mausare nodded. "We will miss you, Brothers. Remember that Drolwym is your home, Habidros. And it can be yours, as well," he said, speaking directly to Donzalo.

"Who knows the future?" asked Habidros. "For now, we are but a little band of soldiers, traveling south to find employment. And when we are done play-acting and you fine fellows," he said, inclining his head toward the four men-at-arms, "make your way home, I may just stay and see what Lama has to offer.

"What say you, Donzalo? Might your father be hiring?"

"With a word from the right person, he might be," replied Donzalo with a wink to the man's brothers.

They camped beside a narrow dirt road, rutted by the wheels of farmers' carts. Around them rose the newly leafing trees, oaks and maples, still visible in the gloaming. The music of a stream in the valley below them could be distantly heard. Habidros chuckled and stood to stretch for a moment.

"Well, boy," said he, "mayhap you should consider a soldiering career yourself. There's little profit in a younger son staying at home."

"Not that you've ever shown much," remarked Guesare, with brotherly sarcasm.

"He has made plenty," said Mausare. "If he could but hold onto it!"

"Ah, yes, rub it in, Brother. Had I saved my coins I might have settled down with an even larger farm than yours." The big mercenary shrugged. "I would be very bored, I think."

Guesare spoke then, more seriously. "Our Donzalo, I think, is meant for bigger things."

For a few moments the men pondered this. Then one of the soldiers broke the silence. "We all know that. Donzalo is a man of destiny." His comrades nodded their agreement.

"That's what everyone back home says," averred another.

And what I have felt from the start, Guesare said to himself. Now all the world will be learning it.

~ ~ ~

Twice, Ansa had gone on stage only to take part in a crowd scene. Each time, she donned a dark wig and attempted to remain shadowed and unobtrusive. None the less, each time she wondered if Jobareth Nafal recognized her.

Her true role tonight had been that of stage manager. From start to finish, Ansa was the one who oversaw this production of 'King Nordoc.' It was an old play, and formal by modern standards, but she had pointed out to Fachalana that it segued neatly into the drama of Oemse that Nafal was supposedly writing — Oemse, of course, having been Nordoc's tragically slain first wife.

Now, they were drawing near the end of the final act. The heroic — and quite dead — Nordoc lay upon his bier, awaiting entombment. At least the ham couldn't overact anymore tonight. Fachalana came to center stage to declaim the closing lines. They were of a rather old-fashioned poetic style, but suited to the young noblewoman's delivery. Their very formality prevented her from emoting too strongly.

Where has gone the king?
Man no more is mighty;
silence spreads its shroud
where heroes sang of old.

Lizards doze upon
the walls of ruined cities;
the wells hold nests of snakes;
the wind rules realms of dust.

Victories forgotten,
sword beside him broken;
the king lies in his grave
and sleeps eternally.

Ansa actually felt moved as the funeral procession slowly exited the stage. Apparently, so did the audience for they applauded loudly and for a quite a long while after the curtain fell. She watched from the wings as the various actors went out to take their bows. Fachalana did so at least three times.

And then, quite surprisingly, her patroness took her by the arm and pulled her onto stage. Despite being a rather petite woman, Ansa was both lithe and well-trained and could easily have broken away. She chose not to.

"May I present the woman behind tonight's production," loudly announced Fachalana. "The talented and lovely Maresta, whom many of you have seen on stage before."

In the front row, Ansa could see Jobareth's eyes grow wide. On an impulse, she smiled and blew a kiss his way.

Fachalana could hardly keep from laughing and did so as soon as they reached the wings. "He will be back here soon," she said. "I have been asked to greet the royal couple and will attempt to take Jobareth with me. That will give you a few minutes."

A few minutes to make my escape, thought Ansa. It's not too late!

~ ~ ~

Jobareth Nafal had no choice but to be patient. Fachalana had, somehow, steered him over to the box where Prince Modareth and his bride waited. A single, seemingly bored attendant ushered them in and tactfully slipped away. Guarding the unassuming prince was neither an exciting nor a demanding duty.

In the mean time, all he could think of was the woman he had known as Posena. No wonder she had seemed familiar. He must have seen her a dozen times on stage!

Ah, but here was his old friend Modi. It been many years since they sat together in the king's gardens, reading passages to each other from favorite books and discussing the mystery that was girls. Then he had gone off to study, leaving his friend behind.

As shy as ever, the prince seemed unsure whether to hug him or shake his hand. Nafal, ever the diplomat, took the hand warmly and then pulled Modareth into a partial embrace. He wasn't sure how much of that was natural to him, now, and how much ingrained from years of training.

Fachalana had no hesitation in throwing her arms around the prince, and his wife as well. "It's like old times, Modi!" she exclaimed, beaming at the group. "How long has it been since we three were together?"

The young man shrugged, seemingly tongue-tied. His wife immediately jumped in, evincing a genuine interest in them and their history. Perhaps nothing she said was of great consequence but that did not matter.

I can see how this is a good pairing, thought Jobareth. He glanced at Fachalana from the corner of his eye to see her doing the same. Both smiled.

"Do come by sometime, won't you?" asked the young prince. "Either one or both." He looked towards his bride. "Th-that's all right with you, isn't it, my dear?" Modareth had largely outgrown his childhood stutter but it occasionally made itself known.

"Of course, husband mine."

Fachalana recognized that her characterization of Carrana as being eager to please was still quite valid. She would welcome any of her husband's friends and do her best to make them her friends. Perhaps it would do well to cultivate this warm, earthy woman.

"Then we will make our goodbyes. We should be getting home." The prince gave his wife a tender look. There was also a hunger in it that both Fachalana and Jobareth noted. Were they surprised? Perhaps, thinking they knew Modareth so well. They were also most certainly amused.

"They are newlyweds, after all," whispered Fachalana as they wound their way through the emptying theater.

"And, I would wager," answered Nafal, "both virgins up until yesterday."

"Hmm, yes, I suppose," murmured his companion. "I suppose." She spoke no more until they reached the backstage.

~ ~ ~

"I am saddened to hear of Lady Vibola's passing," said Ansa. "She was as fine a woman as any I have known. I didn't even mind," she added with a slight smile, "emptying her chamber pot. Well, not too much."

Nafal nodded. "I came to love the old woman," he said, "as did Lomela."

He took another sip of his spiced wine and looked at the two women across the table from him. Then he looked about the little room that served as Maresta's quarters and, apparently, her office as well. It seemed surprisingly spartan, from what he knew of women's bedrooms. She did not live here, he realized; she was only passing through. Was that the life of an actress?

"It seems that there was much I did not know about what happened a year ago. But I still do not understand why my master — your father, Fachalana — wants Donzalo dead."

"Oh, he does not know of the prophecy," Ansa nonchalantly remarked to her companion.

"So it would seem," agreed Fachalana.

Jobareth sighed. "I must resign myself to your whims, my ladies. Might I ask of this prophecy?"

"Our Lady Fachalana learned of it while rifling through her father's papers. She should tell the tale." Though I had already heard of it from my brother, Ansa added, to herself.

"This is a serious business, truly," said Fachalana, becoming instantly sober. She seemed to compose herself for a moment, straightening up her tall frame. Jobareth found himself watching how the light of the lamps fell on her finely chiseled features, her burnished skin. She is truly beautiful, he thought, isn't she?

"The Oracle at Cars made a pronouncement and it was this: that the son of Donzalo would rule in Lama." She was speaking in the measured cadences of the stage. Whether she consciously realized it or not, falling into the ways of the actor gave her the self-control she needed.

"So it is that King Lareth sees him as a threat and wishes him removed. As does my father, though I believe," Fachalana hesitated, albeit slightly, "that he has since found other reasons to hate Donzalo."

The young man let the information sink in for a moment before looking up at the pair. "May I tell Lomela of this?"

"Certainly," answered Fachalana. Ansa slowly nodded her acquiescence.

"Why not another conspirator?" she said with a shrug, though it went against all her instincts as a spy. She had already gone much further than she ever should have. "But as conspirators, we should make plans. We must meet again before you leave Celatas, Lector Nafal."

"Indeed, my ladies. Now, though, I had best be on my way." He rose and bowed to the pair.

"I will walk you out, Jobo," said Fachalana. As her friend went to the door, Ansa took the diplomat's arm, pulling him down to whisper in his ear.

"You and I also must speak again, when we can. There are other matters here — ones which concern our Fachalana."

Jobareth Nafal nodded and followed the Lady Fachalana into the corridor.

5

"I assume Nafal is your creature."

Radal was never certain whether Lord Doufan was obtuse or played games. The man was a sycophant and a sophist, but not to be underestimated.

And he seemed to be one of the few courtiers who evinced no fear of the powerful Lord Radal, adviser to the king and reputed sorcerer.

"These days," he replied, deciding to keep their exchange to small talk, "I believe he is more my daughter's creature."

The man gave him a warm and, Radal suspected, entirely insincere smile. "There have been rumors of a match, my Lord Councilor. Might we expect another wedding soon?"

"Not if young Jobareth is off in Lama with you, my Lord Doufan. I must admit, I do have some hopes for an engagement announcement before you leave."

Doufan noted the 'some.' Apparently the match was far from assured. It would be better to change the subject.

"I hope we can be on the road east, soon. Even I grow weary of these endless parties and balls, Radal." He noted the nobleman's amusement at that statement. "Yes, my lord, I know this is, so to speak, my natural environment." He gestured, arms out, at the festive room in which they stood, surrounded by the elites of Celatas.

Lord Radal nodded. "So it is, Doufan. Let us hope you can be as effective a courtier in County Rosam." He looked seriously upon the man. "It seems you should be able to leave here on schedule. Understand that I expect Nafal to handle the everyday business of your embassy. Your duty is to make that as easy for him as possible."

"In other words, my lord, to be charming? It is my stock in trade."

~ ~ ~

Pol thought no one saw him slip his letter into the dispatch bag. That was all to the good, felt Blen, as he drew it forth. Best that the young fellow suspect nothing.

He had watched the soldier attempting to spy unobtrusively these last few weeks. Whose tool was he? Ah, the missive was addressed to

Nafal. Sir Blen smiled benignly. So Jobareth had asked the boy to keep an eye on things for him. There was no harm in that.

He smoothed the sheet out on the desk before him. The message was short, printed out in large block letters.

Master Nafal, as orderd I write this to you. I have kept watch and all is good here in lama. The Count send a troope of men north. I think they be fetching his boy home. All the castle and the town are talking about Count Borrago and his lady love. There are wagers on the wedding date. I have taken midsummer and hope to win some.

The Princess is well and her son is too but the baby is sick a lot. She look worried when I see her at the keep last week. I watch Sir Blen too but he does not due much. Will keep my eyes open. Pol

Blen read through once more and, with a laugh, folded the letter and returned it to the bag.

~ ~ ~

The Great Road was broad here, and the river ran near at hand. Six men rode south. That they were fighting men, they made no attempt to conceal; the best deception, after all, is that which comes most close to the truth.

They did not hurry, these fighting men. That would attract unwelcome attention and, after all, there was no rush. This was, for the most part, a new country for them. Even Donzalo had never been so far north in his native Lama. So they enjoyed their journey, stopping often. There were plenty enough inns and taverns along the Great Road to take their interest and money.

But they chose to encamp rather than stay in those inns. That was easy enough along these stretches of the Weldar, where forest often grew down to the river's banks. Further south, perhaps, a secluded spot would be difficult to find.

On the second night along that road, Donzalo slept beneath the stars and dreamed a dream. It was an odd sort of dream. Someone was calling to him, he thought, from afar. It troubled him that he could not make out the words. Then the voice faded and he fell into deep slumber.

~ ~ ~

Fachalana was frustrated. She often was, these days. Her attempt at a spell, all on her own, to contact Donzalo's dream-self had not worked as she wished. She could not make herself heard, could not hear him, see him, as she wished.

Yet she had touched him, hadn't she? Was it a matter of practice or would she never have the skill? Little did she realize that her father, powerful sorcerer though he might be, would have been astounded at what she had accomplished.

As he would have been if he knew how much she had learned during their brief link in Donzalo's dreamworld.

Even if Fachalana realized how much she had managed, she still would have wanted more. Her mind, restless as ever, turned elsewhere. She thought of Jobareth and what he had said to her in the theater, of his casual comment on virgins.

Jobareth seemed to assume I wasn't one, she thought to herself. I'm almost tempted to marry him just to prove otherwise.

She sighed. Jobo treated her too much like a comrade. It had always been that way; even as children they had shared rough, boyish games and she the roughest of them all, their ringleader in mischief.

Fachalana liked Jobareth Nafal perhaps better than anyone in the world but knew she would never love him. She wanted something more, someone more, than the men she met here at court. For most of them, she felt contempt. Swaggering idiots!

Could she talk with Ansa about this? Fachalana's courage rarely failed her but the thought of baring herself to her self-possessed friend frightened her. How could she speak of her lack of experience to such a woman?

She seemed very tired. Was this how her father felt after working his magics? Fachalana had witnessed that often enough over the years. She would take a draught and try to sleep and perhaps, just perhaps, she would dream of Donzalo.

THE SHADOW OF ASAK

~ ~ ~

The band of smugglers had turned away from the river, trekking further west to avoid passing through the Rosam territories on this side of the Weldar. Count Borrago's tolls were notoriously high.

"These are the lands of Count Dordos," said Galaro to their traveling companion. Perdos was well aware of that fact, having been resident at Keep Rosam. Dordos ruled over a smaller, poorer county, west and north of Borragos's holdings. It was known that he disliked the Rosam. It was also known that he was in the pay of Sharsh.

Sharsh's couriers were allowed free passage of his lands, aye, and kept fresh horses stabled there, so the latter was not surprising. That other funds, for other purposes, came to Dordos from the king of Sharsh was uncertain but widely suspected.

"There is a spot on the river, north some ten leagues from Rostown, where we will make our crossing. Dordos and his men will turn a blind eye for a small sum. Then," continued the burly Cuddonian, "we will wend north along the Great Road for a while, buying and selling."

"I should leave you when you cross," spoke the knight.

"I assumed as much," replied Galaro. "Where you are headed, I will not ask. Indeed, if it involves my brother, 'tis best I not know."

"Are you noting the band of men headed our way?" asked Perdos.

"I have been watching them for a while. We are well armed and seem matched in number. Still," he said, turning in his saddle and calling out to their troop, "have your weapons ready, boys!

"Always best to be prepared," said he to Perdos.

"Very true. But if they meant us mischief, they would not be riding so boldly," opined the Laman knight.

The other group of horsemen drew closer. Suddenly, Perdos hissed. He knew the man at their head.

"It is Sojel and his cutthroats. They are the ones who seek the death of your kinsman, Donzalo."

"I do not know this Donzalo and care little. Even less than for my brother. But you are under my protection and I do not break my oaths," Galaro stated.

He reined in his steed and held up a hand signaling his followers to do the same.

Sojel's troop also did the same, but bunched up in a much more disorderly fashion. Their sergeant sat his horse for a moment, staring at Perdos.

"Yon deserter belongs to me," he claimed, calmly, flatly, yet with readily evident menace.

"We are honest smugglers," replied the Cuddonian, "and want no trouble. But Sir Perdos is with us and remains with us."

Sojel assessed the group of hard, armed men before him and shrugged. "Very well. It is of no importance." He gave Perdos another long, malevolent look and then led his men past Galaro's party, headed south.

That party kept their hands on their sword hilts till all had disappeared down the road.

"There is a rendezvous point not far from here," said Perdos. "He will be gathering all his men there, I suspect. Far more than he had with him this day."

"Then," said Galaro, "it was Jov's own fortune that we met him this day and not some other."

6

"I, too, miss Lector Nafal and our discussions. There is none other here with his education."

"You two grew close after Donzalo left, didn't you, Brother Grippo?"

"Yes, my lady, though our respective duties and my studies left us ever less time for our talks."

"Oh, yes, your ordination is coming soon," said the Lady Lomela. "At mid-summer?"

Grippo smiled. "All ordinations are at mid-summer, my lady. That is the Kamatian way."

"And I am still a heathen at heart, by Laman standards, aren't I?" Lomela laughed aloud. "I fear I shall so remain, Brother."

"I would not have you change, my lady." Realizing how that sounded, Brother Grippo felt a sudden embarrassment.

Lomela noted this and spoke to him, quite seriously. "Do not be ashamed to be courtly, my friend. It will stand you well in times to come. Jobareth and I both expect that you will rise rapidly in the priestly ranks. Indeed," she continued, "we would not be surprised to see you hierophant here, someday."

"That is something I do not seek, my lady. I do not know if I wish to be a priest at all." He sighed deeply. "It was the only path to learning, in this land. Jobareth has opened my eyes to a greater world.

"Ah, well, I came here, ostensibly, to bless your daughter." He shook his head. "I sometimes doubt the efficacy of my prayers."

"I am sure that prayers are always heard by someone, somewhere, Grippo, if said in earnest. I hope you do not mind that I occasionally address mine to the Lady Esefa."

"That, my lady," answered the acolyte, "is between you and Kamat. And Esefa, too, I suppose," he added with a chuckle. "Let me see to the baby."

"She sleeps in her nurse's room." Lomela's eyes showed signs of tearing up. "I fear she will not live long, Brother Grippo. Please do pray for her, as hard as you can.

"And be sure to stop by here more often. This place has grown cheerless and we could use your company."

~ ~ ~

'King Nordoc' was scheduled to play through the rest of the month, so Ansa was at work each and every morning, attending to business, checking the receipts, making sure the sets were in order — all the details of running a theater and producing a show.

Fachalana appeared when she would. Her friend could not help but note that she often seemed distracted and sometimes quite exhausted. She was worried about Fachalana.

"I think you might use a break, Maresta," came a voice from behind her, as she watched her stagehands repair a painted backdrop. One or another of the cast had leaned too heavily against it last night. None was admitting to it.

"Lector. It is good that you stopped by." She turned away from the workers. "These may or may not keep busy if I leave, but I think it more important that we speak. Will you come to my room?"

In her dressing room and office, she busied herself with the making of tea. Her people were great drinkers of tea, back on the cold eastern steppes, and it was one luxury Ansa was willing to afford herself.

Jobareth sat watching her, waiting. What did he know of this woman? That she cared about Fachalana, he was certain, but there was so little more.

"Would you care for some, Lector Nafal?" she asked, pouring herself a cup. "No? You do not know what you are missing, you and your family with your constant wine drinking."

"Why do you not call me Jobareth? At least in private — I consider you a friend, now, and would have you do the same."

Ansa laughed. "Very well. But I shall not address you as Jobo!"

"Even the Lady Lomela does not use that name for me anymore. Only Lana." His tone became serious. "It is of her you wished to speak, is it not?"

She seated herself across from him and stated her concern

135

outright. "Yes. Did you know she has become her father's apprentice?"

Jobareth slowly drew in a breath. "So that is why you were willing to risk revealing yourself to me." He nodded. "It explains many things. What can we do?"

"Be her friends. Try to guide away from harm, when able. I do not think there is anything more we can do here. Though," said Ansa, "perhaps if we could get her beyond her father's influence for a while, it would help."

"Beyond? Do you mean in Lama?"

"Yes, exactly. If you two were engaged, might she not visit you? And her friend, Princess Lomela, as well?"

The lector gave her a wry smile. "If either of us were actually willing to become engaged.

"Still, a visit might be arranged. The thing is to convince Fachalana that she wishes it. Then nothing will stop her!"

~ ~ ~

Already, Guesare was growing restless. His friend Donzalo, his brothers, all gone from Drolwym, he sat by himself, idly strumming his rebec.

"He will be leaving us again, soon," whispered the Lady Se to her husband.

"Did we ever doubt that?" asked the thane.

Oder had sent his friend a letter. It seemed that the Anian had a spy in the Sharshite capital and, although the details were kept vague, there was much of interest. It was more gossip than aught else, the minstrel realized. Oder would not be giving him serious information in this casual missive.

He had also named a place and time to meet, should Guesare choose to take to the road once more. Coded, naturally, but he understood it. He fiddled a moment with his tuning pegs. It would be good to exchange tunes with Oder again.

It would be good simply to be with Oder, to travel with him once more through the wide, ever-changing world. He knew Oder was not like him, not a man to fall passionately in love with person nor place. He knew he had two wives back in the empire and took casual lovers of either gender, when and where he would. The spy-master Oder was, and would remain, the one who could cast aside anyone and anything, without regret.

Perhaps he should ride to that meeting, a fortnight hence. Would not Drolwym be here when he chose to return? Guesare strummed again and thought on many things.

~ ~ ~

"Silence, my bullies! We don't want them hearing us all the way to Ros-town."

Perdos was impressed by the efficiency of this band. Already most of their goods had been ferried across the Weldar, quickly and quietly. This eastern shore was part of Count Dordos's land; on the far side lay Rosam holdings.

Their bribes — which Galaro claimed went up the ladder to Dordos himself — not only bought them passage but also provided false papers saying that all duties and levies had been paid. Those should get them across the northern border of County Rosam. Landing their freight on the eastern side of the river was the only part that might go wrong. They must not attract attention.

The knight had waited to the last, holding a baffled lantern for the smugglers, and uncertain whether he should actually cross over here with them. That it was not wise to remain on the same side of the river as Sojel, he felt sure, so when the time came he led his horse aboard the final barge. Galaro boarded aside him.

"You will leave us now, Sir Perdos?" rumbled the Cuddonian.

"Aye. I thank you for your company and for your protection." Perdos stared toward the far bank, still hidden in night. "May we meet again in friendship."

And on reaching the shore, he mounted his tall horse and rode into the darkness and away from his traveling companions.

7

"Lector Nafal."

Jobareth looked up from his list to see an attendant holding a diplomatic pouch.

"Ah, the latest dispatches. Thank you." He took it from the man and emptied its contents onto the big marble-topped table. All around the room were boxes and bales, being readied for the journey to Lama. These final preparations were keeping him busy, here in this wing of Lareth's palace.

But not so busy that he couldn't take time to sort through the dispatches — most could be passed on to the proper ministries or to Lord Radal. There was an official report from Blen. He quickly perused it and, finding nothing of great interest or import, added it to the stack of papers for the Lord Councilor's eyes.

No personal letters for him. He wished that Lomela had found time to write but knew she was busy as mother and wife these days, and not so gay since the passing of Lady Vibola. Then he came upon the note from Pol, his young spy.

Jobareth opened the letter and smiled at its message, before holding it to the candle to darken any invisible ink. Yes, there at the bottom.

I know Sir Blen is keeping an eye on me. Best he think me a fool. P

He was glad he had shown that trick to the boy while they had rested at Mountain Keep. Pol was proving more devious than he had hoped and, in this case, Blen seemed the fool.

Nafal looked back over the letter. Lomela's little girl was not well? He had not read that in any official correspondence, including Blen's. It was good to have young Pol at his service, if only to keep him up on matters others deemed trivial.

Now if only all his other plans went as well.

~ ~ ~

"These all seem in order," said the guard, handing back Galaro's papers after a cursory scan. "Did your stay in County Rosam go well?" He was not truly interested but his orders called for him to ask such of all travelers.

"Well enough," answered the Cuddonian. "Well enough. Tell me, sir, is there any news of trouble on the road, armed men or such?" The memory of Sojel's band was still fresh in his mind and Perdos's admonition that it would be growing.

"None. It has been quiet so far this spring and traffic is just starting to pick up along the Great Road. Hmm." He bethought himself for a moment. "There was a little band of soldiers came through here yesterday. Or was it?" He called to the guard on the other side of the border. "Which day did those mercenaries pass by?"

"Early yester-morn," replied the fellow. "A half-dozen of them, heading off to seek employment in the north."

"Yes. They seemed good solid men. Just the sort to have as traveling companions on some stretches of the road."

Probably well ahead of me, thought Galaro. Still, it might not hurt to take this guard's advice and try to catch up to them. "I thank you, sirs. Here is a little something for your trouble this morning," he said, handing each man a small gold coin and leading his caravan through the open border gate.

~ ~ ~

Word at last!

Sojel looked up from the newly-arrived message and out over his growing troop, wondering whether it was time to ride. If he waited, their number would surely increase, but not by much — most of the men had reported and those who had not, might never.

It was odd, though, that Vanob had not appeared.

He reread the paper in his hands. Rumor, it was, not solid intelligence. Still, a chance of catching the Rosam boy on the road was better than idling here.

He turned to the knot of men who stood near him, those he had made his lieutenants. He had little trust in them but they were the best of his mongrel pack. "Get the men ready to move," he commanded. "We are quitting this cesspool of Dordos."

~ ~ ~

"So, all is readied for our delegation to leave on the morrow?" asked Lord Radal.

The man well knew that it was, of course, realized Jobareth. The question was more a statement of fact. "It is, my lord," he answered.

"Very well." The dark nobleman sat, erect, impassive, for a moment, seeming to be more interested in the papers on his desk than the young man standing before him. Then he spoke again.

"Up until now you have been, officially, secretary to the embassy with rank of attache. That is to change." Jobareth tried to remain calm. Was he to lose his post?

"Our Lord Doufan will have his own long-time — and, I assume, trusted — secretary with him. You will need to keep an eye on the man, by the way. We have assigned you a secretary of your own — the young fellow who accompanied you here from Mountain Keep."

"He seemed competent," ventured Jobareth, breathing easier. He was not being sacked, apparently.

"And he admires you," replied the Lord Councilor. "I think he will do well enough, though green. It is to you to see he properly learns his duties."

"I will, my lord."

"I am sure that is true, Nafal. You have done well in Lama, so far." He leaned back in his chair. "Unofficially, you have been acting as our legate, with all the duties thereof but not the authority. We are changing that state of affairs.

"The king and I feel you should be legate in name, as well, still second-in-command to our ambassador, Lord Doufan, but with the authority to act in his name when he is not able." Radal smiled thinly. "Doufan chose not to object, though I doubt he likes it."

Lord Radal held out a document to his protege. "Here is your official appointment. Do not disappoint us, Jobareth."

"I thank you, my lord. Might I ask if Sir Blen's position will change?" It was a question best asked now, though he barely dared speak it.

140

"He will remain master of arms. He will also remain your equal in command, at the king's insistence." Though he allowed no pique to be evident in his voice, Jobareth was certain his master was unhappy about the situation.

Then he decided to broach another subject, most definitely even chancier. "I — I would speak to you of your daughter, sir."

This time, Radal showed actual surprise. "Do so," he commanded.

"My lord, the Lady Fachalana and I have discussed the possibility of marriage." That was certainly true, even if they had not done so seriously. He dove deeper into his semi-deception. "We both feel that, with me leaving for an indefinite period, we should not announce an engagement. That assumes, sir," he continued, attempting to play the hesitant suitor, "that you would approve."

"You know I would, my boy." The councilor paused a moment. "I would not have objected to an announcement at all. I suppose it is too late now, though."

"Perhaps, my lord, you could permit Fachalana to visit us in Lama. The Lady Lomela would greatly love to see her."

"As I recall it," said Radal, "Fachalana rather mistreated the princess when they were children. There were tears and skinned knees and her father's displeasure."

"Which, sir, Lomela and Fachalana remember as great adventures."

The nobleman laughed. "Fachalana sees everything as a great adventure." He gave the young man a stern look. "Be sure she does not lead you into too many.

"And we shall consider allowing her to travel. Now you had best go make your final good byes."

~ ~ ~

Bolos sat with pen in hand. He would trust this missive to no scribe; it was for his eyes only and for those of the king in Sharsh.

The king in Sharsh — not long ago, he had spoken against closer ties with his wife's father. That Lareth had been complicit in the attempts on his brother's life, Bolos had little doubt. But to whom else could he turn now?

He sat back and composed his thoughts. Best he simply tell all his suspicions, lay out each of his grievances to the king. Then, sealed against the prying of spies or diplomats, he would have his own man carry the letter to Sharsh.

Bolos put pen to paper and began writing.

8

"It is done," Jobareth told the two women. "I think he believed me completely."

"You are very much sticking your neck out, Jobo." Fachalana was quite uncertain about this whole scheme. "If our plan puts you in any danger, I *will* marry you. I promise you that."

"You two could do far worse than each other," observed Ansa. Looking into herself, she realized that she liked and admired them both. That was a dangerous thing for a spy.

Indeed, we could do worse, thought Fachalana. But the one reason she had fallen in with this scheme was for the chance to, at last, meet Donazalo Rosam. She would not tell these two that, naturally. What had started as a lark, when she sent Maresta to spy on her friends, had become a much more serious matter to her.

Another might have seen it as obsession.

And in his study, in his villa above the city, Lord Radal wondered if he might, somehow, use his daughter as a weapon against that same Donzalo.

~ ~ ~

The tedium of travel may lead to the wandering of the mind. Donzalo's mind wandered to thoughts of the daughter of Lord Radal.

He still did not know her name. He still wondered if he was meant to seek her. And his recent dream haunted him. He could not shake the feeling that it was connected to her, somehow.

Habidros wondered about his mood. He barely knew the young Laman, it was true, but he did know that the boy had been through much.

And all this talk about his 'destiny.' That would be a load for anyone. Especially if one believed it. The Cuddonian avoided such ideas, himself. It was enough to live and let the future take care of itself.

It always had.

He tried to distract the lad with tales of his exploits in the Siphic states. But it was not his battles that interested young Donzalo; no, it was the city-states themselves, their politics, their sciences. Habidros realized that he actually was not well-schooled on these subjects, despite the years spent fighting the states' wars.

"Is it true that there are no noblemen in the Siphics?" he asked.

Of this, Habidros knew some. "It varies from state to state," said he. "Almost all are republics of some sort, but in one the people will rule and in the next power is concentrated in a few noble families.

"It is true that those nobles keep a low profile and avoid ostentatious display. They fear the people would rise up if they flaunted their positions."

"That," said Donzalo, "may be so everywhere."

"Ha, I suppose it is. From what I have seen of Oles, it is much like the cities of the Siph. Except full of puritanical Lamans rather than the easy-going folk of the east."

"We are not like the burgess of Oles in our county." Donzalo had met and talked with many of them, come down to Ros-town for the fairs. "Though my father," added the young knight, with a laugh, "loves his profits every bit as much!"

~ ~ ~

The Weldar could not be crossed here. He must lead his men further to the north, well beyond the borders of County Rosam, to a morass of swamp and forest and few people. His troop was far too large to go unnoticed anywhere else. Two score they numbered now.

Sojel was not overly familiar with that area. A haunt of bandits and river pirates, he had heard, and the isolated huts of fishermen and hunters. Such should give him no trouble. More importantly, that lawless wilderness also harbored smugglers who would be of assistance in getting his men across. Already had he dispatched messengers to them.

He gave the order now to his lieutenants to move out. Each led a small band, five or six men, so that they might not attract undue attention, with orders to rejoin their comrades in two days.

Whether they would be behind Donzalo's party or ahead of it they would not know. It was not even certain that he was on the Great

Road at all. Sojel could but muster his men on the eastern side and send out scouts to search up and down the highway.

And then, at last, perhaps he could act.

~ ~ ~

Make sure your bearings in what lands you roam:
The wisest man is he who travels far,
Yet keeps his eye upon a guiding star
That someday serves to show him his way home.

"That," said Lord Doufan, "has ever been my philosophy."

Jobareth Nafal recognized the passage, the work of an obscure poet from the previous century. The name of its author escaped him.

He was baffled by this man. The ambassador was full of such quotes and seemed to have a prodigious memory yet not a single original thought in him. At least none that he would share.

Certainly, there was much more to Doufan than he had been led to believe. More than the smooth courtier he appeared on the surface.

Would that the fellow rode, thought Jobareth. They would make far better time. But no, he insisted upon a horse-litter, all the way to Mountain Keep. Probably beyond, as well, on the road to Oles where they would take to the river, passing down the Weldar to County Rosam.

On further consideration, he decided that Lord Doufan was asserting himself. He could ride, no doubt, if he wished. It was his way of showing that he was not to be taken lightly, that he was still the head of this embassy. Jobareth had no intention of challenging that idea nor rising to any bait.

"It seems good advice, my lord," he said. "I have a star of my own." Let him think I speak of the Lady Fachalana, he told himself. It will remind him that I have also a powerful patron. "I shall ride forward and see if anyone knows how far it is to the next inn. My lord." He gave a respectful nod of his head and urged his horse ahead.

~ ~ ~

He could not remain here on the northern borders of County Rosam. There was too much chance of being recognized. Perdos decided to ride due east, up into the hill country and away from the larger villages.

All the way into the wild country that lay between Rosam lands and the Cuddon would he journey, and then swing back to the south, toward the River Abam and Sir Paren's keep. There, he knew the lay of the land. There, he could keep a watch on things and be prepared if the bard Guesare returned.

It would be a hard life, for a time, but he was willing to live on the move, hunting his dinner, sleeping in the open. It would be worth it and, after all, this countryside was a pleasant enough place in the summer.

Perdos bethought him of the inn where he had wintered. He should go back there when this was over, he told himself. Yes, he *would* go back.

9

"You know you can always tell your father you changed your mind, my lady. I dare say he would not be surprised."

"No, I suppose not," admitted the Lady Fachalana. "But it might do harm to Jobareth's career."

"You care greatly for your friend Nafal."

"Yes, Maresta, I do. Too much to marry him, I think." Both women sat a while in silence. "Has anyone ever proposed to you?" Fachalana asked, of a sudden. It seemed an awkward sort of question to her so she felt it best to simply blurt it out.

Ansa considered her answer. She could be more or less truthful if she left out a few details. "Yes, Lana, they have, back home when I was a girl in the countryside." That the countryside of which she spoke was in the heartland of the Anian Empire, she need not mention. "I knew I wanted more. At least before settling down to being wife and mother."

Fachalana hesitated for a moment and then spoke. "I have had more proposals than I can remember."

"Every popinjay in the court sees you as a path to higher position," Ansa observed. "None of them are worthy and you know it."

"Perhaps I should not have kept them all at arm's length." Fachalana sighed deeply. "Have I missed out on too much with my play-acting and self-absorption?"

There is much unspoken here, thought Ansa. Has Fachalana never been with a man? She thought back to the trysts of her teen years, the eager young Ani warriors she had known and loved, to some degree.

But Ansa had become quite the strait-laced young woman since entering her career in espionage. She had taken no lovers in Celatas, choosing to focus on her mission.

"When the right man comes, you will know and let him in," she said, half believing it and knowing it was what her friend would want to hear. "It will happen, my lady."

Perhaps for both of us, she added, to herself.

~ ~ ~

He knew the man. It had been half a year ago but he remembered this knight, leading his men to Sir Paren's manor while he and his mates waited in hiding for an order to attack. An order that did not come when the sergeant decided it was wiser to bide his time.

So what was he doing here on the Great Road, riding north with a handful of men? Surely it had something to do with their mission. Best he get back to Sojel and report.

He mounted up and headed toward the Weldar. The sergeant was a smart one, sending scouts across its stream before the main body of his men. Maybe all had come over the river by now and they could see some action, eh?

The going was difficult here, swampy and uneven, and the Road lay well away from the river, passing in and out of forest where no man lived. A good place for an ambush, he thought to himself. A very good place.

~ ~ ~

He waited beside the road. Another might not have seen him but Guesare was attuned to this land and to those who dwelt in it.

The Prince raised a hand in greeting. "You are leaving," he stated.

"Yes. As much as I love my homeland, I find that I can not abide here long." He swung himself down from his mount to stand beside the fay. "Is that Jola's horse?" he asked. The stallion, all dappled of gray, stood on the ridge opposite,

"He awaits Donzalo's return." The horse turned, silently, and disappeared over the hill.

"Donzalo and I shared a dream. I did not see and understand all that occurred, for it was his dream, not mine. He has told thee of it?"

"No, not a word," Guesare said.

"Then it is not my place to speak of these things. Perhaps your friend will, in time." The Prince's pale eyes met those of his mortal friend. "But of one thing I will speak.

"There was one there who, I believe, did not belong. Only for a brief moment did she enter our vision, but it was enough for us to sense her presence, and she ours.

"She was much like Jola. I think she must be her sister."

"Lord Radal's daughter? Ah, so that is why the boy was asking me about her!" Many small things came together to form a whole in the minstrel's mind.

The Other nodded. "Then he recognized the kinship as well. Perhaps this, too, is a part of his destiny. We do not know.

"This we of the fay do know: the woman is growing as a sorceress. We have felt her new-found but still undisciplined power from afar. It is very great, though it will never rival that of our Jola." The Prince paused for a moment, as both mortal and fay remembered their loss.

"Her name is Fachalana," he continued. "Do with this knowledge what you will. I know only that Donzalo is your friend. Care for him.

"I bid thee farewell and fortune upon your journey."

~ ~ ~

Habidros slid one long pistol from its holster. The other lay ready at hand on the other side of his saddle. "Those are fighting men headed our way. Be on the lookout, lads."

Shielding his eyes from the afternoon sun, Donzalo scanned the approaching group. Then he laughed and spurred his steed forward. "Captain Corgos!" he called out.

"Master Donzalo!" the soldier hailed him.

Habidros relaxed and slipped his gunne back into its sheath. He cantered up to the pair. "That would be Sir Donzalo now," said he, "and well deserving of it. You ride from Castle Rosam?"

"That we do, sir. I am Corgos." The knight held out his hand in greeting.

"Habidros, late of Drolwym," said the Cuddonian, taking it. "You have come to fetch our young friend home, I would assume."

"That would be so, Sir Habidros. 'Tis already late in the day. Let us encamp here and take council." It was rough country, and wild, lying at the northern edge of swamplands. Corgos swatted at a mosquito. "And let us build a good fire to keep these pests at bay. We passed through clouds of them this day!"

As the darkness of a spring evening fell upon them, the men of both parties circled a roaring fire. It was only in part a deterrent to the swarms of biting insects.

"I rode these lands when younger," said Sir Corgos. "Save in the cold of winter, such are always about.

"As are," he continued, "brigands. It is not a good section of the Road to travel without protection."

"It would seem well suited to ambushes," observed one of the Cuddonians, to nods of agreement all about.

"Well, with both our troops riding together, any bandits will likely choose to leave us alone," said Habidros, "but it is not such that concern us. Those who seek Donzalo's life may not be easily discouraged."

"You intend to ride south with us?" asked the Laman captain.

"We swore to accompany him home and we will do so."

"Then our lucky thirteen shall begin the journey to Castle Rosam in the morning," declared Corgos, slapping at his neck.

~ ~ ~

Sojel pondered his scout's report. Behind him, his men were mustering on the river bank, all safely across the Weldar. It had gone well, some small payments, some intimidation, and a pair of smugglers' skiffs were put at his disposal.

Those smugglers prepared now to row their boats home. At the sergeant's signal, a pair of his ruffians ran their swords into them and let the bodies slip into the dark Weldar's stream. Best no one be left behind to tell tales.

"Pull those skiffs up into the bushes and hide them, lads," he called. They might come in handy if they needed to cross back.

Sojel could think of but one reason this captain of Count Borrago should be riding north with a half-dozen men. He was going to fetch the boy back to his father.

And if he went, he must surely return. They could wait right here in this wild land and ambush them. A rare smile came to the man's face.

It was not a smile you would have wanted to see.

10

"You would treat with Orgelo?" Bolos asked of his father. He paced back and forth across the small tower room, obviously ill at ease with the idea.

"That I would," replied Count Borrago, "if only so Sharsh does not take us for granted. And do sit down, won't you?"

The younger Rosam plunked himself into one of the plain wooden chairs, pulling irritably at his short tunic where it had creased beneath his leg. He knew Sorsen, son of Count Orgelo, had ridden in earlier that day. Why had he not been informed of the visit?

Borrago noted the expression on his son's face. "County Arvaram is not our enemy, Bolos. Our rival, aye, and often opposing us on policy, but between us we keep the peace in Lama. That is a delicate balance and one we must take care not to upset.

"Anyway, Sir Sorsen's presence is not as his father's representative." Though we will most surely speak on matters of import, the count said to himself. "He has traveled here to do business in the town and comes to the keep only out of courtesy. And to discuss armor with our master of arms, undoubtedly," he added, chuckling.

The mention of Sir Copago did nothing to improve Bolos's mood. Indeed, it made him only more suspicious. Why should his father's bastard be spending time with the heir of Orgelo?

What if he sought his support in an attempt to usurp him?

Bolos told himself he had done well to write to the king in Sharsh.

~ ~ ~

"They come!"

What? So soon? He had barely brought his contingent to the road, much less had time to plan an ambush.

"Where?" Sojel asked the scout.

"Barely a league north of us when I saw them. Half that by now." The man climbed down from his lathered mount. "It looked to be a dozen men and the Rosam boy among them."

More than he had expected. Still, his forty should be be enough,

with the element of surprise on their side. He quickly called his lieutenants to him, pointing out where he wanted them to position the
men. No, not across the road from each other, idiots! Do you you
want them shooting their own fellows?

Five men with matchlock muskets. Group them over there and let
none reveal themselves until they had loosed a volley. Any man who
showed himself prematurely would be flayed alive, yes, and his leader
with him.

Then they waited but not for long. Indeed, they had barely
concealed themselves when they heard the clopping hooves of
approaching horses.

Two-by-two they rode, eyes wary and scanning the roadsides. A
doughty group of men, thought Sojel, gripping his pistol. Not the
sort to run from their duty. This may not be easy.

Then he blew his whistle and the muskets blazed.

~ ~ ~

Galaro knew this stretch of road. He had done business here more
than once.

He knew also the dangers of it and warned his followers to keep a
sharp lookout. Would that they had caught up to that band of
soldiers that went before them!

He would not have minded the company of Sir Perdos, too, if that
man had chosen to remain with them. The Laman knight might not
be much of a talker but his sword arm would make up for it.

But the fellow was obsessed with his revenge. That his brother
Guesare was disliked here and there, Galaro was not the least
surprised. He had never gotten on well with him either. Oh, he
should admit it, he had bullied him terribly when they were young.
The Cuddonian regretted that, for the most part, but never let it
bother him.

This was more, of course, than mere dislike. Guesare had slain
the man's brother. A fair duel, Galaro had heard, so such hatred
puzzled him a bit. It must go deeper.

He turned his attention back to the road. It was rather marshy here and too open on either side for concealment. There was thicker forest ahead, if he remembered aright.

Those traveling mercenaries had been more than a day ahead of him and had remained so, according to those he had asked along the way. A train of pack-horses could only move so fast.

He thought again of his brother and then of his ancestral home of Drolwym. It had been long since he had seen its haphazard towers rising from the hills of the Cuddon. Maybe he would go back someday.

Not this year. Too much business to attend during the summer. And who would want to winter in the Cuddon, with its fogs and chill winds?

Then, from not far ahead, came the sound of musket fire.

~ ~ ~

Lord Radal looked over the missive before handing it back to Lareth.

"Do we take this seriously?" asked the king.

"We must," replied Radal, "even if his fears are baseless."

"Do your spies have anything to say of the situation? I know you have men in Lama that report only to you." If he did not trust so thoroughly in the loyalty of his friend and councilor, he might not be willing to countenance that.

"The reports are — conflicting. Different men read situations differently, depending on their own biases. I shall instruct our agents as to what occurrences and situations they should be alert." Lord Radal paused. When he spoke again, his voice seemed barely under his control, a rasping whisper. "I hope to have news — good news — shortly of our other concern with that family."

Lareth gazed long from the window before speaking. A mist of spring rain obscured the city below him.

"And if your minions fail you again?"

"Then, my king, I may just go there and tend to it personally."

154

11

One man had fallen in the first volley. Another was thrown from his stricken mount but rose to his feet, unharmed. The smoke and stench of gunpowder hung in the air.

Then the horsemen broke from their cover, charging the small band.

In the open, the seasoned soldiers could have withstood the attack of this rabble, aye, even outnumbered by more that three to one. Here, there was no room to maneuver, to mount a counterattack. It was man against man, sword against sword.

Sojel discharged his pistol and was pleased to see another man reel. Then he plunged into the battle, saber in hand. Straight toward Donzalo Rosam he rode.

Corgos drove his steed between the two. Blade rang on blade and then the foes were separated by the maelstrom of battle. "To me, men!" rang out the voice of Habidros. "Stand united!"

A half-dozen or more of the attackers lay dead or wounded, mostly fallen to pistol fire on their first charge. There would be no time to reload, now, on either side. The musketeers had left their weapons and entered the fray with drawn swords.

It is not only men who count in such a fight; horses matter as well. Donzalo's defenders had not only the better skills and weapons but also the superior mounts. Their heavier warhorses could push through the nags opposing them, allowing their riders to come together around their captains and the man they protected.

"Should we run for it?" gasped Corgos, hacking at an opponent.

"It's our best chance," came the reply from Habidros. "Go!"

The group urged their horses forward, hoping to break through and away from the attackers. Too many men, too many swords, slowed their progress. Another of the Cuddonian men at arms fell from his saddle to be trampled beneath the milling hooves.

~ ~ ~

Doufan was stretching his legs, walking alongside his litter for a few minutes. This meant the entire entourage must slow down to his pace.

I might as well dismount too, thought Jobareth. It felt good to be out of the saddle briefly, to work out his riding cramps. His horse, seemingly, appreciated the change as well.

"It's not much further, my girl," he told her. The Royal Road climbed through pine-clad foothills now and the pass at Mountain Keep lay but a couple days travel away. He should write some letters while they rested there, to his family, to Fachalana.

To Lomela, as well. Any message would reach her far sooner than he would personally. It would be slow progress through Lama with Lord Doufan, who wished to spend time with his fellow ambassador in Oles.

Jobareth Nafal recognized the importance of such a visit. The burgess who ruled that city would certainly wish to know what a new embassy in County Rosam might mean for them, to be reassured that no secret treaties were being planned between Sharsh and Count Borrago. Doufan was just the sort of man for the job.

I don't really have it in me to fill such a position, do I? he asked himself. I'll always do my best behind the scenes.

And that, after all, is where true power lies.

~ ~ ~

Galaro took in the situation with a glance. He and ten of his men had ridden hard up the road, leaving the remainder of the troop to guard their train.

Bandits, he assumed, attacking fellow travelers. There was no question as to the proper course of action — any outlaw band operating on the Great Road was a danger to him and to his own business. Drawing his pistol, he spurred forward, his fellows close on his heels.

As a battering ram shatters a dry-rotted door did they shatter Sojel's rag-tag force, driving deep into the heart of the battle. The ruffians who opposed them saw their sure victory become suddenly uncertain and had not the courage to stand, breaking and running in all directions. There were those who did not make it to the cover of the woods.

In fury, Sojel watched his green rabble disappear, before doing so himself.

"Well met, Brother!" came a voice from behind Galaro.

"Habi?" He wheeled his steed about to face his sibling, only a year younger than he and his companion on many a boyhood adventure. "Well met, indeed!" he roared.

~ ~ ~

Ansa nibbled her pen tip. She did that when she was not sure what to write.

Oh, now I have to sharpen it again, she told herself, and took a dainty but quite sharp knife to the quill's end.

"Dearest Brother," she started. Well, that's a good beginning anyway.

She had already sent ahead her usual report, mostly full of rumor and overheard bits of gossip. There had not really been much of import to send along in some time.

No, this was to be a more personal message.

"The big news," she wrote, "is that F. may cross the mountains later this year." Hmm, she thought, I'd better explain that better, and crossed it out.

What I should do is tell the whole story of Jobareth and Fachalana and the prince and everything else that has gone on around here. Yes, all of it.

And she put pen to paper and began writing.

12

"So you have been behind us all the way from Ros-town, Sir Galaro?" asked Corgos.

"More or less," replied the burly Cuddonian. Almost from Ros-town it had been. "We had hoped to catch up with you. It seems we did, at last!"

"You might as well have the horses and arms left behind," said Habidros. "I know you cherish your profits, Brother." There were several captured mounts, with their harness, and a number of dead whose bodies had been stripped of aught of value before being tossed into the swamp. Galaro's men went about that task quite efficiently.

"Ha, profits are in part what kept us from catching up, I reckon. We did have to stop and trade here and there along the way. Although," continued Galaro, "we intended to do most of our business further north."

"Why not ride back south with us now, sir?" Donzalo asked. "It is not long till May Festival and the Spring Fair."

"We had intended to be back in your father's lands for the Midsummer Fair, lad. I will speak of it with my fellows. Though I may lead them, we are a free company of traders and must vote on such decisions.

"Now, how stand you and your men? You have taken casualties, I can see." Galaro's men had come away from their charge largely unscathed.

"One of those who accompanied us from Drolwym lies dead and another sorely wounded," reported Habidros.

"Two of mine are slain, as well," Captain Corgos said. "The rest are all fit enough to ride, though several of us bear wounds." He held up his own bandaged arm. "We are fortunate we did not lose more."

"We would, I think, have lost all our lives were it not for Sir Galaro," observed Donzalo. "I regret that I am the cause of this."

"Ah, yes, Perdos told me these men sought your life." He noted that several present knew the name. "It is not my business as to why.

"Let us finish clearing things up here and then we can encamp down the road with the rest of my crew."

~ ~ ~

There was nothing to be done about it. His attack had failed and the boy would make it home before he could mount another. Best to break up his troop for now. What was left of it.

Fewer than a score had made it back to the banks of the Weldar. Some lay dead, Sojel knew, or wounded. Others would have fled, choosing their direction at random. Some of those might find their way back in time and some of them would choose not to.

He would get this bunch back across the river and disband, for now. Let them get south as they will and regroup later. Another handful boarded one of the skiffs and pushed out into the stream.

As for the sergeant himself, he would have to report all this and then await his master's instructions. Best he head straight for Mountain Keep.

~ ~ ~

A great bonfire lit up the camp. Some of Galaro's men had broken out instruments, flutes and hand drums and small lutes, and brightened the gathering the more.

"Your wounded man will need to be borne in a wagon," Galaro whispered to his brother. "I would not see a fellow Cuddonian, indeed, a retainer of our father, receive less than we can offer him. Whichever way my company goes, we will take him along."

"I thank you, Brother," replied Habidros. "I would truly welcome your company on the journey south. Perhaps your protection, too, if the need again arises. I have no doubt," he added, with a smile, "that the count's gratitude might prove profitable as well."

"It's unlikely you will be attacked again, don't you think? Your enemies have scattered and the Great Road grows safer as you ride toward Keep Rosam. But it would be good to ride together again."

He rose and gestured for his men to gather round him. They conferred for no more than a minute or two, with much nodding of heads and glances toward their guests. Then Galaro turned and spoke.

"We ride south with you, gentlemen. Let us be on our way in the morning."

AFTERWORD

I hope you have enjoyed this, the second book in the saga of *Donzalo's Destiny*. The story begun in 'The Song of the Sword' is continued in 'The Sign of the Arrow' and concludes in 'The Hand of the Sorcerer.'

This fantasy novel is set in a world and time of its own, although it most closely resembles 16ᵗʰ Century Central Europe. The stories and characters, the world in which they "exist," arise from ideas I have played with for many years.

Incidentally, if one wishes to pronounce the names in this book, it is generally safe to treat them as one would Spanish — at least the names that come from the widely-spoken Muram language.

Stephen Brooke

Author and artist Stephen Brooke lives and works in an old farmhouse in the Florida Panhandle. *The Shadow of Asak* was his ninth book.

The *Donzalo's Destiny* epic fantasy
by Stephen Brooke consists of four books:
I. The Song of the Sword
II. The Shadow of Ask
III. The Sign of the Arrow
IV. The Hand of the Sorcerer

All are available from Arachis Press, a small publisher dedicated to presenting meaningful literature for readers of all ages.

Visit http://arachispress.com for our catalog.

www.ingramcontent.com/pod-product-compliance
Lightning Source LLC
Chambersburg PA
CBHW030516260626
47157CB00005B/1768